# THE PEACE-TIME PEPPER GIRLS

## (Lexie and Nancy embrace peace-time)

by

# SANDRA SAVAGE

ISBN: 978-0-9931332-8-2

# Acknowledgements

Dedicated to the memory of my wonderful son, John
McGlashan, who left this world on
10th January 2018 at the early age of 50 years.
Till we meet again.

# Also by Sandra Savage

Annie Pepper

Annie Melville

Annie MacPherson

The Pepper Girls

The Pepper Girls at War

The Dark Heart of Roger Lomax

The Green Years

# Chapter 1

"Is it finally over?" Annie asked as she poured out their morning cup of tea.  It would soon be Christmas again and for the first time since the war had begun in 1939, people were tentatively hoping that 1945 would bring peace and healing back to Dundee and its people.

"Yes Annie," Billy assured her, "it's all over and Lexie and Ian are both safe and well."

Annie sipped her tea and watched as Billy Dawson handed her the Courier newspaper.  "They're beginning to bring the men home," he told her, pointing to the latest news from the Government "and we'll see Ian and Lexie again soon."

It had been three years since Billy had ended his marriage to Josie, after finally admitting his love for Annie and when she confessed her love for him too, she had made him the happiest man in the world.  Their love for one another had begun over forty years ago in Ireland when, unknown to Billy, Annie had conceived their son, giving birth to him in the Poorhouse in Belfast. Despite all the pain and hurt that had visited them since that time, their love had endured and was now stronger than ever and their son John Adams was now a Doctor of medicine, like his adoptive father.

Billy kissed Annie on the cheek.  "Time and tide waits for no man," he said, "and nor does Baxters Mill."  He pulled on his jacket from its resting place on the back of the chair and cast a loving look over his wife.

"Will you be seeing Isabella today?" he asked, "or maybe Nancy could do with a visit from her favourite Aunt."

"Nancy, I think," Annie said, pushing her chair back from the table and following her husband to the door, "maybe she'll know when Billy will be demobbed."  Billy Donnelly had been in the thick of the fighting in France with his regiment of the Scots Guards and despite some close calls, he'd be coming home unscathed, at least physically.

For a while it had looked like Nancy's marriage was broken and beyond mending, thanks to Billy's involvement with a local prostitute, Gladys Kelly, but since the birth of his second son, Kevin and with Nancy's  father and Annie's help and guidance, they had both realised that their bairns were what mattered and seemed to have made a fresh start.

"Remember I love you," Billy whispered as he kissed Annie goodbye "and that everything will be alright."  Annie nodded. After her late husband Euan had been killed by one of Hitler's bombs, that had exploded in Baxters Park in 1942, she had wanted to die too, but her sister-in-law, Isabella, had pulled her through and now, by some miracle, she had found happiness again with her first love,  Billy Dawson.

"And I love you," she whispered back "and I'll let Nancy know her dad is thinking about her."

Annie listened as Billy's footsteps descended the stairs before returning to the kitchen.  The weather outside was turning wintery, as she began to fill a wicker basket with goodies for Nancy and the bairns.  Since the birth of Kevin, Nancy had had to stop working as a Weaver and with only her husband's Army pay coming in and three mouths to feed, Annie's visits were always welcome.

She wrapped six scones in a tea towel, added the last jar of raspberry jam from the batch she'd made in the summer, along with a bag of oatmeal and some of Harry Duncan's pork sausages left over from Sunday's dinner. She slipped in a poke of Grannie Sookers for good measure for Nancy and two bars of chocolate for Mary Anne and wee Billy from her sweet ration. Kevin, or King Kevin as Lexie had named him when he was born, would settle for sucking on one of the biscuits Annie took from the biscuit barrel to have with their cup of tea.

Nancy still lived in the two cramped rooms off Victoria Road with her brood, but when Billy came home, it was going to be so overcrowded that Annie didn't know how they were going to manage.  There was word that a house building programme was going to be starting on the outskirts of Dundee, but that seemed a long way off and with barely enough money to pay the rent for their two rooms in Victoria Road, Annie knew that Nancy wasn't holding out much hope for being able to afford anything bigger.

Annie buttoned her coat and pulled her hat tightly on her head before picking up her basket and heading off to her niece's home.  Her sister Mary had given birth to Nancy when she was married to Billy Dawson and since Mary's death from Tuberculosis when Nancy was still a child, Billy had made sure she was looked after and loved, despite being brought up by Mary's second husband, Joe Cassiday, also now gone.

"Cooeee," Annie called as she passed the kitchen window, on the way to Nancy's door.

"Come in, Auntie Annie," Nancy called back, "the door's open."

King Kevin was crawling around the floor, chasing a rubber ball that kept bouncing away from him every time he tried to grab it and Nancy was piling some coal onto the fire in the grate.

"Come away in," Nancy smiled, "the kettle's nearly boiled and you'll soon get warmed up.  Annie took of her hat and coat and began emptying the basket.

"You're so kind to us," Nancy said, "I don't know how we'd manage without your baskets.

Annie nodded in acknowledgement, "any word from Billy about when he'll be home?"

"Not yet," Nancy replied, "but with Mary Anne now working in the Callander at Baxters and wee Billy learning the painting and decorating with Ernie Griffiths, their wages have helped to replace some of the loss of mine. Which is just as well," she added, "once Billy's demobbed from the Guards, his money will stop too."

A look of weariness brought a frown to Nancy's pretty face, now showing lines of worry and fear for the future.

"But enough about me," she said, forcing a smile back onto her lips, "what's happening with Lexie and Ian? Any word about when they'll be back home?"

Annie laid the scones on a plate and uncapped the Raspberry Jam. "Well, Ian should be home soon, but I don't think he'll be here for long."

Nancy poured out their tea. "How so?" she asked.

"I think he's quite smitten with a girl from Carlisle he met at one of the army camps and, although he doesn't say much, I think there's marriage in the air and he'll be going to live with her in Carlisle."

"And Lexie," Nancy queried, "how are things with her?"

Annie's face became bleak. "You know Robbie was killed in action barely a month after they married?" Nancy nodded, one minute she was congratulating Lexie and Robbie Robertson on their marriage and a few weeks later, Lexie was a widow.

"Well, Wing Commander Johnson at Lossiemouth, re-enlisted her back into the WAAF," Annie continued, "and she saw out the rest of the war there."

The two women were quiet as they each considered Lexie's future.

"Will my dad get her back working in Baxters Office when she's home?" Nancy asked.

"Annie shrugged her shoulders, "it'll depend on Lexie," she said, "maybe too many memories for her to cope with, back in Dundee, but if it's what she wants, then your dad will make sure it happens."

The visit was interrupted by Mary Anne returning for a dinner-time bite to eat. "Auntie Annie," she cried, throwing her young arms round Annie's neck, "did mum tell you I'm a working lassie now, earning money to help out till dad comes home?"

Annie hugged her back, her wrinkled skin rough against the smoothness of Mary Anne's young face.

"You're a clever girl," she said, "and there's a wee bar of chocolate for you in the basket for afters."

Annie watched as Mary Anne munched on her cheese sandwich, the smell of the jute mill wafting round her turbaned head. How much water had flown under the bridge since she herself had been a naive young girl in Ireland along with her sister Mary, protected by their own dad and mum and safe from harm.  But her father's death had changed all that and Billy Dawson's appearance at the farm soon after to help with the flax harvest, had awoken a deep love for him that time had never managed to erase.

Half an hour later, Mary Anne was off again, back to the Mill with a cheery smile and a sparkle for life in her eyes.  "Soon be Christmas," she called out as she passed the kitchen window.

Nancy shook her head as she swept King Kevin into her arms, when he had crawled too near the fireplace.  "That girl," she said, smiling, "never fails to make me laugh, she's so full of fun and energy sometimes I think she'll burst."

Annie tickled Kevin under the chin.  He was so like his dad, he couldn't be denied.  The apple hadn't fallen far from the tree that was for sure, Annie mused, thankful that all that business with Jim Murphy and Nancy was now history.

"I'll best be on my way," Annie said, setting her hat back on her head and slipping her arms into her coat.  "Your dad says he'll visit soon, but if there's anything you need you've only to ask." The two women hugged. "I'll let you know when that husband of mine returns from the war," Nancy said, "then we can get back to being a family again."

Annie was glad to hear her niece speak so happily about the future and she crossed her fingers that Billy Donnelly would feel the same way.

# Chapter 2

The shock of Robbie's death at sea when a torpedo had hit his ship, The City of Glasgow, with the loss of all on board, had almost broken Lexie.

Wing Commander Johnson was in the process of completing the paperwork for Lexie leaving the WAAF when the news had come through to him from Lexie's mother. He'd thought she had been on her way to marry the Canadian flyer, Captain Rainbow McGhee and was shocked to hear the news that Lexie had married a Merchant Navy Captain from her home town of Dundee instead. However, the death of the man, a month later, had been worse news and he had put Lexie's paperwork on hold until he'd had the chance to contact her directly, so it was with almost fatherly concern that he'd read her letter.

*Sir*

*I believe my mother notified you of the loss of my husband, Captain  Robertson, however, I have given my future careful thought and I feel that remaining in the WAAF to help fight and defeat Germany is the path I wish to follow.*
*As I am no longer married, I would respectfully request that the termination decision be put aside and you allow me to remain at Lossiemouth on active duty.*

*Sergeant A Melville*

Of course he'd complied with the Lexie's request.  Her bravery in the rescue attempt of the crew of the ditched

Wellington Bomber that had earned her the Empire Medal and her conduct in dealing with the death of her step-father had been evidence enough for him to know that she would do her duty and be a credit to the WAAF.

Lexie, read again the Wing Commander's response and her mind drifted back to that terrible time when the only thing that had got her through the grief of losing Robbie, had been the discipline and support of the Lossiemouth men and women of the air force and especially Wing Commander Johnson.

But now, the war was over and at 32, Lexie was now packing her bags for the last time and returning to civilian life in Dundee.

Her best friend, Winnie Adams would be back home in Montrose Lexie reckoned and Sergeant Brady would be heading home to his family. Lucy Ashford, Lexie's fellow WAAF and confidante, had married the Canadian pilot, Brad Hollis and gone to live in Canada.

Lexie sighed, three years ago, she had been on her way to marry Brad's fellow Canadian and Squadron Leader, Captain Bo McGhee, but Robbie Robertson had changed all that when fate, on the journey to Canada to marry Bo, had guided her to Robbie's ship, bound for Halifax, where the love they'd had and lost, blazed back into life and when he'd asked her to marry him, she'd had no reservations about saying yes.

Lexie could feel her throat tighten as the news of Robbie's death was replayed in her mind. Their future had been so bright then, despite the war and for a short time, they had been the happiest couple in the world.

Lexie packed her belongings into her travel bag and forced her thoughts back to the present. There was no going back, Hitler and his submarines had seen to that. The only way was forward and that meant going back to where she had begun, Dundee.

Lexie took a last look round her quarters, before heading for the door. Everything neat and in order, her single metal bed made up and ready for inspection, her desk cleared of all paperwork and her chair neatly placed in front of it. It was almost as though she'd never existed in this place. But despite everything she had experienced, she knew that joining the

WAAF had been the best thing she had ever done and giving it all up now, filled her with trepidation.

Annie and Billy Dawson were preparing for Lexie's arrival.

"The train gets into Dundee at quarter past four," Billy said, "provided it's on time, of course."

Annie pushed the net curtaining aside and looked anxiously at the sky.

"It looks like snow," she said worriedly, "do you think it's snowing in Lossiemouth?"  Billy's arms circled her waist. "C'mon worry-boots," he said, "everything will be fine and Lexie will be home by teatime."

Annie turned to face him.  "Are you sure?" she asked, "what if......"

Billy pulled her closer.  "Sssshhhh!" he whispered, "I'm sure."

Annie relaxed in his arms.  Of course everything would be fine, she told herself and if it wasn't, Billy would fix it.

"I'll get my coat and hat," she said, smiling now.  "I think Lexie deserves a happy face at the station......after what she's been through........" Annie had begun to add, her voice suddenly fading at the memory of Robbie's death "....and that's what she's going to get," she decided, determination returning with the words.

Billy nodded.  "I'll get the motor started and we'll give Lexie the biggest welcome home anyone's ever had."

Lexie leaned against the window of the railway carriage transporting her back to Dundee.  Memories of her time at Lossiemouth, fought for attention with her short marriage to Robbie, as she tried to come to terms with the hand that fate had dealt her.  So much happiness had been hers but then it had been cruelly snatched away and there was nothing left for her, but to shoulder her burden and carry on.

The squeal of the locomotive's brakes and the rush of steam heralded her arrival at Dundee West Station.  She knew her mother and Billy Dawson would be waiting and, for their sakes, she had to put on a smile along with her coat and hat. Lexie stepped onto the platform and looked around.

There she is," Annie murmured, already tears threatening to fall.  She waved a gloved hand as Billy manoeuvred her through the rush of people around Lexie till suddenly, she was there in front of her daughter.

"Lexie," Annie whispered, "you're home at last," as she gathered her daughter into her arms.

Annie could not have chosen any more meaningless words for Lexie if she'd tried, as she hugged her close. She looked over her mother's shoulder to where Billy stood waiting and with a small shake of her head, told him all he needed to know. Lexie may be home, but she wouldn't be staying.

Lexie fixed a broad smile on her face as she extricated herself from her mother's hold. "And it's good to be home," she said, "it's a long journey from Lossiemouth."

Annie linked her arm into Lexie on one side and Billy on the other.

"Now the two most important people are here, I know the war is definitely over," she said, forgetting to mention Ian, who she felt was his own man and no longer needed his mother, but Lexie, she confirmed to herself, still needed her.

The drive back to Albert Street was taken in the gathering gloom of late afternoon in Winter and Lexie watched the scene go by with growing apprehension. She couldn't go back to this, she knew without doubt, Dundee with its memories and grimness was the past and Lexie felt she still had a future to live and not just exist in.

The motor jolted slightly as Billy pulled on the handbrake. "Everybody out," he called, trying to bring some levity into the deepening darkness.

The trio made their way into the close and up the stone steps to the front door. Lexie took a deep breath as she followed Billy and her mother into the lobby and felt again the stillness of the past surround her. If only Robbie had lived, returning to Dundee would have been so different. Their love for one another would have swept her above the mundane and the for-off lands he'd talked about would have seen them in the summer sunshine, the scent of Lavender and oranges filling their nostrils instead of the pungent smell of jute.

The kitchen table had been laid ready for her arrival, the centre-piece of which was a Victoria Sponge, sprinkled with icing sugar and surrounded by plates of sausage rolls and tiny sandwiches.

Lexie felt a pang of guilt as her mother bustled around the kitchen, making the tea and chattering nervously about the day to come, when Billy was planning a homecoming party for both Lexie and Ian to enjoy.

How she wished Ian was here now to take some of the pressure off her shoulders. Lexie had been through three years of war, but it was nothing compared to the stress she was feeling now to conform to her mother's will.

"Is Ian expected home soon," she asked?

Annie placed the teapot on its trivet on the table. "Soon, I think," replied her mother almost absently, "but I don't think he'll be staying long," she added, "seems he's met someone in Carlisle and will be going to live there once he's demobbed."

Lexie felt her hands clench on her lap. So Ian wasn't going to be a buffer for her, she was going to have to go through all of the reasons why she had to leave home, yet again. But, that was for another day, right now she would accept she was back where she began and begin to plan her departure again, and soon, starting with a visit to Sarah Dawson, Billy Dawson's eldest daughter with Josie McIntyre and Lexie's best friend.

—-—oOo—-—

# Chapter 3

Billy Donnelly was going home. Demobbed from the Scots Guards along with his fellow warriors, he tugged at the sleeves of his demob suit which were at least two inches too short for his long arms. The train journey was interminable and even the banter between the other men in the carriage failed to ignite any excitement about returning to civilian life.

Since Mary Anne's accident, Nancy had become more like a wife again, but three more years had passed since then, with only the compassionate leave when Kevin had been born to remind him of Nancy and home. Her letters had been all about their new son and little about how she was missing him, so when he'd received a letter from Gladys Kelly saying how much she wanted to be with him again, his thoughts had returned to the prostitute and her willing body.

He removed her letter from the inside pocket of his jacket and read it again.

*I know I'm not proper, like your wife, but no one could love you more than me. If you ever think of me kindly, then I'll be waiting and hoping you'll knock at my door again.*

He ran his finger over Glady's address. Lochee, he smiled, and not far from his mother and father's house. He closed his eyes and tried to imagine their meeting up again. It wasn't hard to do. Gladys still aroused an urgency in him that he couldn't deny and for the rest of the journey home to Dundee, he thought of her and not Nancy.

"Look efter yirsel' Billy," the Scottish voice of one of his comrades shouted, shaking him awake and bringing him back to the present. Billy looked out of the carriage window at the grime of the railway station. "Are we here?" he asked, "Dundee?"

"We're here," said the soldier, "and if you dinna get yirself aff this train, you'll find yirsel' in Aberdeen."

Billy grabbed his suitcase from the overhead luggage rack and followed the other men onto the platform. The doors slammed and the Station Master waved his red flag and blew his whistle. With a belch of steam, the train eased out of the station and moved forward, up the East Coast to Aberdeen, disgorging returning soldiers, sailors and airmen back to their homes and families as it went.

Billy lit a cigarette and never felt so alone. No loving wife to greet him, no familiar faces to welcome him home, just strangers and echoing emptiness. He patted his jacket pocket. One person loved him and as soon as he could, he would be at her door.

"Can I give you a lift home Billy?" a familiar voice asked from the shadow of a station pillar. Billy screwed up his eyes, as the form of his father-in-law, Billy Dawson took shape.

He stepped forward, his hand offered to the young man.

"Welcome home," Billy said, "Nancy's home with the bairns and she can't wait to see you again."

Billy Donnelly eyed his father-in-law with suspicion. "I think I can find my own way home, thanks," he said dryly, making to walk off, but Billy Dawson had other ideas. He had to make Billy see that his place was with Nancy and his family and this might be his only chance to speak to him alone.

"There's a lot of water flowed under the bridge since we last met," Billy said, "and I want you to know that I want nothing more than to see you and my daughter happy again."

Billy Donnelly said nothing, but nodded towards the station exit.

"Right," said his father-in-law, acknowledging Billy's consent, "the motor's just outside."

Billy had taken a long time and a lot of visits to his daughter to make sure she knew the importance of marriage and family and now it was her husband's turn to hear the same words. He knew that Billy was now a full-grown man and a seasoned fighter to boot, but somewhere inside him, he knew that he had a weakness and that weakness was Gladys Kelly and it needed to be stamped out, if Nancy and the bairns were to have any future.


Billy steered the motor into Dock Street, but instead of turning up Whale Lane into Blackscroft and King Street, he continued out towards the Stannergate.

"Has Nancy moved then?" Billy asked, fixing his eyes on his father-in-law as he drove.

"No, Billy," he told him, "Nancy's still in the two rooms in Victoria Road.

Billy frowned. "So where are we going then?"

"You'll see," came the enigmatic reply, as his father-in-law stopped the motor at a row of fishermen's cottages lined along the shingle beach and overlooking the river.

The older man scrunched over the gravel towards a wooden bench near the water's edge, followed by his confused son-in-law.

Billy Dawson took out his cigarettes and offered the soldier one, lighting it with his lighter which flickered in the cold breeze.

The young man inhaled the tobacco smoke and squinted at the grey water of the River Tay and the outline of Fife on the other side of the estuary.

"So........what are we doing here?" Billy asked.

"There's something I want to put to you," Billy said "if you want to listen, that is?"

The two men locked eyes, the younger of the two blinking under the stare of his father-in-law. Despite having had to face death on the battlefield, Billy was still afraid of Nancy's father and the power he wielded in his life.

"Have you given any thought as to how you'll keep your family fed, now you've been demobbed?" Billy asked evenly.

The young man pursed his lips and flicked the end of his

cigarette into the wind.

"That's my business, I think," he replied, feeling his muscles tense.

Billy took a deep breath, trying to get alongside his son-in-law hadn't gotten any easier with the passage of time, but Nancy's future was at stake, not to mention that of the bairns.

"Nancy may be your wife, Billy," Billy Dawson replied through tight lips, "but she's my daughter and I want the best for her and the bairns which, if I'm not mistaken, she won't get with an unemployed ex-Scots Guard from Lochee."

Billy felt his fists tighten, but remained silent.

"So, here's what I'm proposing," his father-in-law continued, "and it's not up for debate."

Billy almost laughed at the preposterous situation he found himself in,

"and if I don't agree?" he asked, "what'll you do, take your belt to me?"

It was beginning to look like a Mexican Stand-off. This wasn't good and Billy Dawson knew it.

"No," he said evenly, "if you don't agree to what I'm about to suggest, then it'll be Nancy and the bairns who'll suffer and I won't let that happen."

Billy Donnelly, stood up and thrust his cold hands into his trouser pockets, knowing he hadn't anything to offer his wife other than scraping a living in the Mills, if he was lucky.

"I'm listening," he said.

Billy Dawson stood up and began walking towards the cottages, his hand clutching an iron doorkey.

"Here" he said, stopping in front of the one storey house and handing the key to his son-n-law. "Open it."

Billy frowned as he took the key and unlocked the door. It led into a large room with a flagstone floor and wooden beams holding up the ceiling. There were windows at either side of the room and an open fireplace was centred against one wall. Billy indicated a connecting door and followed as Nancy's husband went through into a passageway where two more rooms opened off the narrow space.

"There's a kitchen with a range to the other side of the parlour, and a garden where Kevin can play and Nancy can hang her washing to dry."

Billy took it all in, wondering all the time what it meant for him and for his future with Gladys Kelly. Lochee was a long way away from the Stannergate.

Without asking if he liked it, Billy continued with his plan. "This is for Nancy and the bairns, where they can live in fresh air and away from the mills and the grime."

Billy turned to face his nemesis. "And where do I live?" he asked, "I'm an unemployed ex-Scots Guard from Lochee remember, I can't afford to live here!"

Billy lit another cigarette, but didn't offer one to his son-in-law this time.

"You can afford to live here," he said, "when you're an under-manager at Baxters."

So, that was it, Billy realised, his father-in-law would have total control over his life, if he agreed. He felt the strands of fate begin to tighten around him. His every move would be monitored by Billy Dawson, at work and at home. Nothing had been left to chance and he knew for certain that he was damned if he didn't agree and damned if he did. Gladys Kelly and her warm body were being put well out of his reach and both men knew it.

"Does Nancy know about this," he asked. Billy shook his head, "I thought I'd give you the pleasure of telling your wife how much you love her and how wonderful your life together will be when you all move to the Stannergate."

"You win," Billy said, his voice heavy with resignation, "is there anything else you want me to do?"

Billy Dawson's eyes levelled with his son-in-law's. "No," he said, turning to go, "get back in the motor and I'll drop you off at Victoria Road."

Billy knew there was no point in arguing, he'd been well and truly caught and trudged behind his, soon to be boss, at Baxters.

The drive back into Dundee was taken in silence until they arrived at Billy's home.

"I'll expect you at half past seven on Monday morning ready to work," Billy said, "and don't be late."

He pulled the motor away from the kerb and smiled. Nancy would have a new home, her husband back and earning and Gladys Kelly would become a thing of the past, never to be mentioned again.

Billy Donnelly watched as the motor disappeared down Victoria Road, nodding softly to himself as he turned to climb the stairs to his future. There was more than one way to skin a cat, he told himself, and Gladys Kelly was one alley cat he couldn't forget.

# Chapter 4

Lexie knocked gently on Sarah's mother's door. This was the first time she had confronted Josie since Billy Dawson had left her and married her mother.

She flinched in shock at the sight of Josie who peered around the crack that had opened, as she inched the door back. Her hair was grey and flattened into her head in a tight bun and her skin sagged around her neck and eyes. Lexie remembered her as a lovely woman, who had sparkling eyes and a generous smile of welcome anytime she had visited before the war, but it was obvious that life had taken its toll on her countenance. She hadn't aged well.

"Mrs Dawson?" Lexie said, shakily, "Is Sarah in?"

Josie Dawson's eyes widened, as she realised who was asking.

"No she isn't," came the sharp reply, "and I don't want the likes of you darkening my door again."

"Who is it mother," Sarah's voice sounded in the background, getting louder as she came to the door and peeped over her mother's shoulder.

"Lexie!" she squealed in delight, "come in, come in."

Lexie's hand fluttered to her neck, "I don't think it's a good time" she stuttered, "your mum......"

Sarah turned her mother to face her. "It's alright mother," she said, "I'll just talk to Lexie for a wee while. Go back inside and get yourself a cup of tea."

Josie drew a dark look at Lexie before turning back into the gloom of the lobby.

Sarah grabbed her coat from the hallstand and quickly pulled the door closed behind her.

"C'mon," she said, "let's go somewhere where we can catch up," her eyes bright with happiness.  "It's been too long," she said, grinning widely, "but now you're back, things will be alright again."

Lexie wasn't sure what Sarah meant by that, but followed her down the stone stairs out into Morgan Street and across to a small Tearoom in Albert Street.

They ordered tea and scones and once they'd been delivered to their table, Sarah clasped Lexie's hand in hers.  "Now," she said, "tell me all about what's happening, are you going back to work at Baxters and oh! I'm sorry.....I forgot about Robbie."  Her whole posture changed, "I heard all about it from your mum, I'm so sorry......"

"Whoa!" Lexie said, "I know I'm back, but it's not for long," she said, kindly, "I'll be moving on again, just as soon as I find a way back out into the world and away from here."

"But, you've only just came back to us," Sarah whispered, a bleakness coming into her eyes.

Lexie leant back in her seat.  "Back to us?" she repeated, feeling her gut tightening at the thought. "I'm back, yes.....but not to stay," she added again, more firmly than she'd meant to.

"Oh," Sarah murmured, spooning sugar into her tea and slowly stirring the brown liquid.

Lexie looked at her friend more closely, noticing her shoulders had drooped slightly and her lips had quivered and tightened.  The picture of Josie at the door returned to her mind. Was this Sarah's life now, she wondered, living at home with her mother and working as an English teacher at Morgan Academy.

Lexie shuddered.  If she stayed in Dundee, her life would be much the same as Sarah's, living at home with Billy Dawson and her mother and working at Baxters Mill Office again. A wave of compassion hit her for Sarah's plight and she could see why her arrival had brought so much hope to her heart.

"Do you want to tell me about it?" Lexie asked gently, "how things are with you, I mean?"

Sarah's eyes met hers. "I'm 33 years old, Lexie," she began, "my two younger sisters are both married with children of their own and I teach English to girls who couldn't care less about grammar and syntax and since.........." Sarah took a deep breath, "since dad left and married your mum, mother's gone from being a somebody to being a nobody."

"But surely, that's not your fault, or mine for that matter," Lexie said, "sometimes life knocks you for six and when that happens, you either sink or swim."

Sarah stopped stirring her tea. "It's alright for you," she said, her voice heavy with resignation, "you don't have to spend every evening trying to keep hopeful that, one day, things will change for the better and I thought.....well, I thought that you turning up again might be the change I've been praying for to get my life back on track."

Lexie had been hoping that Sarah would have been the one to console her but instead, it looked like her friend was in a worse state than she was!

"Look," Lexie said, fastening on a bright smile, "maybe I won't be around for long," she said, "but at least while I'm here, let's make the most of it and have some fun." Sarah returned a weak smile back.

"Fun?" she asked, "I've almost forgotten what that's like."

"Well," Lexie continued "the war's over now and the boys will be back home soon and there'll be plenty to do to get things moving again, so let's cheer up and do our bit to help."

Sarah smiled albeit tearfully, "and can we go dancing again?" she asked, tentatively, remembering the evening long ago, just before Lexie had enlisted with the WAAF, when they'd gone to the Palais and how much she'd enjoyed the music and the male attention.

"Of course we can," Lexie assured her. In fact, let's do just that this weekend."

The smile faded from Sarah's eyes. "But what about mother," she said, "she'd never let me go out with you and especially not to the Palais."

Lexie could hardly believe her ears. Sarah was 33 years of

age and still needed her mother's permission to go out!  What had happened to her during the last five years when the war had taken over their world? Whereas, Lexie had blossomed and grown in independence and confidence, Sarah seemed to have withdrawn from life into her safe world and, Lexie felt sure, right where her mother wanted her.

She felt the strands of the past tightening around her again, if she wasn't careful, she'd be drawn back into the existence she had fought so hard to escape from.  She felt worried for Sarah, but even more worried for herself, she had to find a way out of Dundee and fast, before it was too late.

—-—oOo—-—

# Chapter 5

Nancy was the first to react when she heard her husband's footsteps coming along the flagstones and stopping at the door. Her heart was beating furiously, as she threw the door open and rushed into Billy's arms.

"Welcome home," she said loudly, hugging him tightly before turning to summon the bairns.

"Look who's here," she called, "dad's home from the war."

Mary Anne and wee Billy stood grinning sheepishly at their mother's show of affection and King Kevin toddled over to the towering figure of his father and clutched his leg.

Billy bent to pick him up. "Hey, wee man," he said, "how's the King of the Castle?"

Nancy beamed.  This was what she'd dreamt of for so long, her family united once again and her husband back where he belonged, with her.

All of that nasty business in the past with 'that dreadful woman' as she called Gladys Kelly, was over and done with, her father had seen to that and now, they could get on with being a proper family again.

Nancy guided Billy to his armchair and knelt down at his feet. Carefully, she untied the laces of his boots and slipped on a brand new pair of men's slippers.

"There," she said softly, "they fit perfectly."

Mary Anne and wee Billy, nodded vigorously in agreement while Kevin continued to try to climb up his father's legs. Nancy straightened and lifted the toddler away and handed him to Mary Anne.  "Your dad's just in the door," she said, smiling, "maybe you and Billy could take Kevin for a wee walk, while I get his tea ready."

Mary Anne nudged Billy, who was about to protest at being seen out with a toddler, "we'll take him down to the swings at Blackscroft," she decided quickly, "he can sit on my knee while Billy gives us a push."

Their coats were pulled on and Kevin's woolly hat was unceremoniously plonked on his head. "See you later dad," Billy called over his shoulder" and welcome home from me too."

The little trio headed out into the cold day and waved as they passed the kitchen window. "Mind crossing the roads now," Nancy cautioned Mary Anne, pushing aside the net curtain, "keep hold of Kevin's hand at all times." Mary Anne waved and nodded and then they were gone.

Nancy filled the kettle, her mind working over-time. Had her father spoken to Billy about the cottage at the Stannergate and the new job, she wondered? Of course, she wasn't supposed to know, but her fears about the future, when Billy would be demobbed, had forced her father to give her advance news of his plans.

She handed her husband a cup of tea and settled in the rocking chair on the other side of the hearth.

"I'm so happy you're home again Billy," she ventured, longing to find out what he thought about her father's proposals.

"Good," he said evenly and without emotion, "but it may not be for long."

Nancy almost dropped her cup. What was he talking about, she panicked, he was home to stay and they'd move house to the lovely little cottage at the Stannergate and he'd be an Under-Manager at Baxters and they'd live happily ever after..........wouldn't they?

"I don't understand," Nancy said, confusion and fear lacing the words.

Billy put his cup down on the tiled grate. "I'm going to re-enlist in the Guards," he said, "it's good money and there won't be another war for a while, so it'll be a doddle."

"But......" Nancy managed to splutter, "what about us, the bairns.....they need their dad to be here...and so do I."

Billy wanted to feel something for his wife, but even faced with her desperation, he felt nothing. He knew his father-in-law too well. Move him away as far as possible from Gladys Kelly and give him a job where he can be watched and his comings and goings monitored. Well, he wasn't going to wear that particular cloak and, although he loved his bairns, he loved his freedom more and that included being free to see Gladys.

His time away at war had seen his wife taking up with a 'fancy man' Jim Murphy and a man didn't get over these things lightly, he'd repeatedly told himself, as his anger at Nancy became replaced with indifference. Billy kicked off the new slippers and replaced them with his boots.

"Where are you going?" Nancy asked in disbelief.

"Out," Billy said, "give Jim Murphy a chance to get you into bed again."

Nancy clutched her throat with shock. "But, that was a mistake," she said wildly, "it meant nothing...."

Billy turned his back to her. "And Gladys Kelly meant nothing to me," he said, flatly, "so when you and your father get over her, I'll get over Jim Murphy."

Nancy slumped back into the chair as the door closed behind him.

He knew! Nancy realised. All of her father's plans to keep her husband away from Gladys Kelly and at home with her, had been rumbled and to blame her fling with Jim Murphy, for his lust for the prostitute, was almost too much to bear.

Shakily, she rinsed out the cups at the sink, her mind and heart racing.

How could he, she fumed, her wonderful future crumbling to dust at Billy's reaction to her father's plans. She now knew, for sure, that he'd spoken to her husband and she also knew for sure that her dad was the only one who could do anything to change Billy's mind.

Her thoughts raced back to the day Billy had found out about Jim Murphy. She still didn't know who had told him but she had never seen him so angry when he thought Kevin had been fathered by Jim and not by him. But he must have known Kevin was his when he was born though, he was the spitting image of Billy.  Had her fling with Jim Murphy really been the cause of Billy's decision?

Was there really no love left for her in Billy's heart?

Nancy felt her eyes well up.  She had put so much faith in her dad's ability to fix everything, but this time, it seemed that even he had failed.

She looked at the clock, it had just gone three, her father would still be at work at Baxters and the bairns wouldn't be back till teatime.

She donned her coat and hat and hurriedly locked the door behind her.

She took the steps down William Lane two at a time and was out of breath by the time she reached the offices at Baxters.

"Can you tell Mr Dawson that his daughter is here and needs to see him?" "It's a matter of urgency," she added, taking a seat in one of the chairs in the hallway as the Receptionist telephoned her father's office.

"I'm afraid he left earlier today" she said, replacing the receiver, "he's not expected back in the office till tomorrow."

Nancy grimaced. "Thanks," she said, turning to leave more slowly than she'd arrived.  Maybe Billy will have changed his mind, once he's had a chance to think about things, she told herself. "Please let him understand," she whispered softly, otherwise........

# Chapter 6

Lexie's encounter with Sarah had left her shaken. Her worst fears had been realised. Life in Dundee wasn't for her, no matter how easy her mother and Billy would make it for her. She'd seen too much and experienced too much to return to the mundane existence she had lived before joining the WAAF.

Annie was in the kitchen, baking enough scones and cakes to feed a regiment, when Lexie came in.

"You're back," she said, smiling broadly, "there's a Maderia Cake cooling on the rack and I know it's one of your favourites." Annie began filling the kettle, her whole being seemed to have grown lighter with her daughter's return and she hummed, tunelessly, as she set the cups in their saucers.

"How's Sarah?" she asked, suddenly aware of Lexie's silence.

"Not good," she replied, "in fact, since........Billy left her mother," she didn't add 'and married you' "her life seems to be spent just existing in a world of coping with her mother's bitterness and teaching English at the Morgan."

Annie stopped making the tea and pulled up a chair across from her daughter.

"And, she blames me, I suppose?" Annie stated.

Lexie said nothing.

"So, you think I'm to blame as well, do you?"

Lexie sighed. "I don't think anyone's to blame," she said, quietly, "just like it was nobody's fault that Robbie was killed, it just happened. War's like that."

The lightness that Annie had been feeling was rapidly disappearing, with the realisation that, although her daughter was back in body, she wasn't back in spirit.  The war had done more damage to Lexie than was obvious at first sight.

"I know that you probably don't want to hear this, but Josie knew when she married Billy that it wasn't a love-match.  She loved him, but that love wasn't returned and they lived a marriage of convenience, that gave Josie the respectability and security that she needed and it gave Billy the same."

Lexie nodded tentatively.  She'd always loved her mother, but had never asked her if she was happy with her lot.  Euan seemed to have met her needs, but now she wasn't so sure and wondered if Billy would have left Josie if Euan hadn't been killed and her mother widowed. Had Billy really loved Annie all that time, she wondered, and she, him?

"Anyway," Lexie said, feeling the conversation wasn't helping.

"Sarah's life isn't going to be mine."

"That's a strange thing to say," Annie ventured, "you're nothing like Sarah and despite what you think, I'm not the cause of Josie's or her unhappy life."

Lexie shrugged.  "What I mean is........" She was about to say that she would be leaving Dundee as soon as humanly possible, when the front door clicked open and Billy came into the kitchen.

If he sensed an atmosphere he didn't show it, he was too full of his meeting with Billy Donnelly and his plan for Billy and Nancy's future, to notice that Lexie and Annie were tense.

"Something smells wonderful," he said, tapping the Maderia Cake.  He turned to Annie, "is there any tea going," he said, "I'm parched."

Annie returned to the tea making, glad of the excuse to leave the table and not hear any more accusations from her daughter.

"How's your day been Lexie?" Billy asked cordially, but before Lexie could reply Annie jumped in. "She's been to see Sarah," she said, feigning brightness, "catching up on things, like girls do."

"Good," he said, biting into his slice of Maderia Cake Annie had placed in front of him, "and I've had a pretty good day myself," he added mysteriously.

The two women turned their attention to Billy and, for the time being, focussed on him.

"Well," Annie said, nodding to Lexie, her curiosity peaked, "tell all."

Billy licked his finger and mopped up the last crumbs of cake from his plate before continuing, building the interest of his audience.

"Billy Donnelly's been demobbed," he said "and I met him at the station earlier today."

"That was nice of you," Annie commented aimiably. She was glad Billy was back safe from the war and now, he and Nancy could get down to the business of rebuilding their marriage. Euan had been alive at the time of the 'incident' that almost broke up the family and, in his role of Police Sergeant, had been the one to have spotted Nancy and Jim Murphy coming out of the Palais arm in arm and obviously besotted with one another. And, when Billy had found out that not only had Nancy been unfaithful, but that she was also pregnant, his anger had become almost murderous. Fortunately, when King Kevin was born, it was plain that he was Billy's flesh and blood, but had too much water flown under the bridge for their marriage to survive? Annie wasn't sure.

"But that's not the best part," Billy was now saying, bringing Annie's attention back to the present, "I've persuaded him to move Nancy and the bairns to a rented cottage in the Stannergate and to start work at Baxters as my Under-Manager."

Billy sat back with a satisfied smile on his face.

Annie digested the news. "But that's wonderful," she said, "and Billy has agreed to all this?"

There were a few moments of silence before Billy replied.

"Not in so many words," he said, "but he'll agree to the move and the job if he's wise.......for the sake of Nancy and the bairns, if not for himself."

Lexie felt a frown forming above her eyes. "If he's wise?" she echoed.

Billy focussed his attention on her, as the rebel in Lexie rose up, her expression balking at anyone being told what to do.

"No one's telling him what to do Lexie," Billy said, in a voice that brooked no further discussion, "I'm just helping him and Nancy get back to being a family again."

Annie felt a frisson of tension forming in her neck and shoulders. Billy Donnelly and his obsession with Gladys Kelly had caused Nancy many a sleepless night, but with Euan and Billy's help, it had looked like he'd returned to the 'straight and narrow'.  Maybe her husband was just making sure it stayed that way, she reasoned.  Only time would tell.

Lexie pushed her chair away from the table before anymore could be said.  She'd liked Billy Donnelly and felt that Nancy wasn't the sweet little girl that her father still seemed to believe her to be. She'd also seen Nancy at the Palais with Jim Murphy and there was nothing innocent about her behaviour then.

"Maybe I'll drop in and see Nancy tomorrow," Lexie said, leaving the table, "take a lollipop for King Kevin."

That'll be nice," Annie said "and take some of these scones for Nancy as well, they'll only go stale if they're not eaten."

The heaviness that had been returning to Annie since her conversation with Lexie was deepening.  It wasn't her fault that Josie was bitter, she told herself, when she had chosen to marry Euan all those years ago and Billy had wed Josie. And they'd all been happy with their choices, hadn't they?

She poured more tea into Billy's cup.  "Why did you leave Josie?" she asked bluntly.

Billy lit a cigarette and eyed his wife.  "You know why," he responded, inhaling the tobacco smoke. "Why do you ask?" he countered.

Annie gazed at her teacup.  "Just something Lexie said."

"And what exactly did Lexie say?"

Annie took a deep breath.  "Sarah blames us for the state of her mother's health and so, I think, does Lexie."

Billy took Annie's hand in his.  "For many reasons, Josie was never happy in our marriage and neither was I and nothing could be done to change that.  Leaving her was my decision and letting me back into your life was your decision and I thank God for that, but none of it was your fault Annie, none of it."

Annie felt her chin tremble.  How could love be so wonderful but at the same time be so hurtful.

"Are you sure?" she asked Billy, "really sure."

Billy took hold of her other hand and helped her to her feet.

"I'm sure," he said, wrapping his arms around her and holding her close to him. "Josie is a troubled soul," he said, hoarsely, "and had to blame someone for her unhappiness and that someone, was me."

Annie nodded into his chest.

"C'mon," he said, "let's take a walk to Baxters Park, before it gets too late, blow away all these unhappy thoughts and remember, that we love one another and that's all that matters."

# Chapter 7

By the time Billy had downed his third pint in the Thrums Bar, his mind was beginning to harden. Who did Billy Dawson think he was, he asked himself, to tell him how to run his life, where to live and where to work. He'd starve before he took anything from his father-in-law, especially if it involved him not being able to see Gladys Kelly.

Going home to Nancy wasn't an option, but visiting Gladys Kelly was.

He pushed the empty beer mug away and looked at the clock above the bar.  If he took the tram to Lochee, he could be knocking at her door by seven o'clock.

"Nice to see you again, Billy," the barman smiled, as he picked up the empty mug.  "Glad the fighting is at an end and you boys are back home," he nodded gratefully.  He'd been too old to go to war, but his two sons had been conscripted into the Black Watch. Only one had survived.

Billy acknowledged the man but said nothing, coming home isn't all it's cracked up to be, he wanted to say, especially when you have a wife who's a slut and a father-in-law who's set on keeping you tied down to her.

All thoughts of Mary Anne, wee Billy and King Kevin were pushed to the back of his mind as he boarded the Lochee tram and were replaced by images of Gladys and her warm body welcoming him back.  She didn't ask for anything from him, no demands, no money, no responsibilities, just to be with her, as and when he could.  He closed his eyes as the tram rattled towards Lochee and he felt his muscles tense as his desire for her began to rise, yes, Gladys Kelly was his and his alone, despite being a prostitute, she would always be his alone.

A light was glowing in the window of Gladys's single-end home as Billy entered the close leading to her door. The war had seen its winners and losers and Gladys had been one of the winners. Dundee had been flooded with servicemen from far and near and the demand for her services had reached an all time high. Not only had she done very well for herself, she was now the Madam of a Brothel in an ex-boarding house in Polepark in partnership with local bookie Michael Flannaghan.

"Wha's there," she called out, wearily, on hearing the knocking at her door. She'd given herself the night off and was in no mood to 'entertain' another client.

"It's me," the deep voice responded, "open up."

Gladys felt a shimmer of recognition run through her. "BILLY?" she asked, shakily, hurrying to open the door.

It had been a long, long time since she'd last seen him and was sure he'd forgotten all about her, but NO, he was here and standing in front of her looking more handsome than ever.

"Have you missed me?" he whispered, stepping into the room and closing the door behind him.

Gladys felt her eyes well with tears. Unable to speak, she nodded.

"Then show me," Billy said, almost harshly, as he pulled her towards him and wrapped his arms around her.

Wordlessly, he lifted her up and carried her to the bed in the alcove of the room, months and months of pent-up lust washed through him as he pulled her blouse open exposing her breasts and neck. Well-versed in the ways of sex, Gladys welcomed him in, just as he liked it, he was back in her bed at last and, this time, she was going to make sure that was where he stayed.

Nancy was pacing the floor of her little home, her eyes keeping flicking to the kitchen clock. She'd hurried back from Baxters, more agitated than ever, her fears for the future mounting by the minute. If only her father had been at work, he would have reassured her that all would be well and she would have been able to relax. And the bairns, she wondered anxiously, where were they? It was getting on for five o'clock and they hadn't come home from the swings at Blackscroft yet.

The loud banging at her door made her jump.  At first, she thought it was Billy coming back, but quickly realised he had a key and didn't need to knock.

She hurried to the door.  "Mrs Donnelly?" the policeman asked.

"Yes," Nancy replied, anxiously, real fear gripping her body, as the unknown reared up in front of her.

"Is your husband at home?"

"No?"

The police constable removed his helmet.

"Can I come in?"

Nancy stood aside, her face white and her knees trembling.

"I'm afraid I've a bit of bad news, Mrs Donnelly," he said, motioning for her to sit down.

"There's been an accident, I'm afraid......."

"ACCIDENT?" Nancy quivered.

"Your wee boy, Kevin Donnelly, has had to be taken to the DRI....."

Nancy thought she was going to faint as the policeman continued, "he was playing on the swings at Blackscroft and as far as we're aware, he tipped backwards and fell from the swing, landing on his head."

Nancy leapt up and grabbed the front of the policeman's tunic.  "Is he alright," she gasped, "and Mary Anne and Billy, where are they?"

"Hush now," the officer said, "they're all at the DRI, they went in the ambulance with him, but I can't tell you any more than that."

Nancy reached for her coat and quickly pulled it on. "I need to get to the Infirmary," she said, the fear for her children putting her into a blind panic.

The policeman returned his helmet to his head.  "There's a police van and driver downstairs and he's been instructed to take you to DRI."

Nancy nodded and followed the policeman out onto the landing, pulling the door closed behind her.  "Where can we contact your husband, Mrs Donnelly?" he called to her disappearing back. But Nancy didn't respond. She didn't know where her husband was, she just knew he wasn't where he should have been, with her.

The drive up Infirmary Brae to the hospital didn't take long and Nancy ran through the entrance into the hospital, the adrenalin fuelling her flight.

"Hud up there missus!" a male voice said, firmly, stopping Nancy in her tracks, "calm yirsel' now and tell me whaur you want to go."

Nancy's arms were held in a firm grip as she looked into the kindly eyes of a Hospital Porter.

"It's my wee bairn," she said, breathing rapidly, "he's had an accident and he's been brought here. I need to get to him," she added desperately, "please, tell me where he is."

"Ah'richt dear," the porter said, instantly understanding the situation, "follae me."

They hurried along the main corridor before turning into the Admissions Office. "Wut's yir bairn's name?" the porter asked Nancy.

"Kevin Donnelly," she told him, her eyes wide with fear.

He spoke quickly to the nurse on duty, who nodded and came out of the office. "Mrs Donnelly, I presume," she said. Nancy nodded acknowledgement. "Kevin's been moved to the Children's Ward," she said, briskly, "follow me."

Mary Anne saw Nancy as soon as she came into the Ward and rushed towards her, her face white as a sheet and her eyes red with crying.

"He fffell," she stuttered, "I told him to just sit still on the swing while I tied my shoelace, but he tried to swing himself and toppled........." Mary Anne burst into a new flood of tears.

Nancy gathered her in and joined wee Billy standing at Kevin's barred cot and gazing down at the toddler.

Kevin's eyes were closed and a large bandage covered his head. Nancy felt her heart leap as she reached out to touch his skin. A wave of relief washed over her as she felt its warmth. He was only asleep, not dead, as she'd first feared.

Wee Billy was a picture of dejection. He'd been the 'man of the house' while his father had been away at war and he'd let everyone down when he was needed. All he'd had to do was keep an eye on Kevin, while Mary Anne fixed her shoelace, but instead, he'd been watching two of the big girls on the swings, hoping the wind would blow their skirts up over their knees and.......on seeing his mother, his shoulders slumped even further. He wasn't a man, he was a failure and his father would blame him for it all.

The nurse squeezed Nancy's shoulder. "I'll tell the doctor you're here," she said quietly, "he'll explain everything."

Nancy nodded her thanks and motioned for wee Billy to come into her arms. The show of forgiveness brought tears to her son's eyes. "I'm sorry," he murmured, "it was all my fault."

"Ssshhhh now," Nancy told him, "it was nobody's fault, everything will be fine," she tried to reassure her son, but her heart was in her mouth, as she gazed at the stillness of Kevin.

"But dad," Billy insisted, "he'll blame me for not looking after him......"

Nancy felt her lips tighten. If anyone was at fault, it was her husband, if he hadn't been so stubborn......! "No, he won't," she said, bringing her attention back to wee Billy, "he knows accidents happen, even when we're careful."

The nurse and the white-coated figure of the doctor came down the ward toward Nancy. "I'm Dr Morton," he said, "is it Mrs Donnelly?"

"It is."

"And these two young people are also your children?"

"Yes." The doctor smiled at Mary Anne and Billy.

"Would it be alright if they went with the nurse and she'll give them some tea while we have a chat?"

Before Nancy could agree, the nurse was already gathering them and steering them towards the ward door.

Nancy was offered a seat by Kevin's bed as the dividing cloth screen was pulled over separating them from the rest of the ward.

"Is you husband not with you?" the doctor asked.

Nancy clenched her fists, "he hasn't been demobbed yet," she lied.

The doctor understood and nodded. He'd seen what the war had done to so many families and just hoped that Kevin's father could be contacted.

"Mrs Donnelly," he began, "your son's had a really nasty bump on the head and he was unconscious when the ambulance men got to him."

"But, he'll be alright, won't he?" Nancy interrupted, fearful of what the doctor was telling her.

Dr Morton leaned towards her. "Head injuries, like Kevin has had," he said, carefully, "can't be predicted, I'm afraid, so I can't say how he'll be, till he's fully awake."

Nancy felt her blood run cold.

"And......when will he wake up, properly?" she asked, her whole being now trembling with shock and fear.

The doctor cleared his throat. "He's in what is called a Coma," he said sombrely, "and until he comes out of this Coma, we won't know if there's been any damage done to his brain."

Nancy turned her disbelieving eyes towards her son. "But, he looks like he's just asleep," she said, willing Kevin to open his eyes."

"And, hopefully, he'll come round soon and all will be well," Dr Morton said, trying to reassure Nancy without giving her false hope, "but until then, we'll look after him and it would be advisable if you could contact your husband and let him know what's happened."

"I don't know where he is," Nancy said, her emotions threatening to overwhelm her, "but my dad can be telephoned. I know where HE is."

If the doctor sensed any bitterness in Nancy's voice, he chose to ignore it. "If you tell me his number, I'll get the nurse to telephone him right away."

Nancy had never felt so alone in her life as she gently stroked her son's hand. She could forgive her husband's refusal to let her father help them, but she would never forgive his absence at their son's bedside in his and her hour of need."

—-—oOo—-—

# Chapter 8

The telephone rang as Annie was fetching her coat and hat.

"I'll get it," Billy called to her, "probably a problem at the Mill."

He picked up the receiver. "Mr Dawson speaking," he said.

He listened in silence as the formal voice told him the reason for the call and it wasn't a problem at the Mill.

"Tell my daughter I'll be there right away," he said, replacing the receiver just as Annie came into the room.

"Your daughter," Annie said "was that about Nancy?"

Billy helped her on with her coat, his actions calm but his mind racing.

"It was the DRI," he said holding onto her arms as he said so, "wee Kevin's had an accident," he told her, "Nancy's with him but Billy's not, she's alone.........again," he added angrily. Would the man ever be there for his daughter when she needed him, he fumed, right from the start, he'd been nothing but trouble and after his offer of a home and a job, Billy couldn't believe that he had gone AWOL again.  If he was sniffing around that prostitute again.......Billy felt his anger deepening......he'd swing for the man.

Annie hurried after Billy to their motor car, neither of them able to speak but fearing the worst.  The Infirmary loomed above them as the car pulled up the steep approach.  "Nearly there," Billy muttered almost to himself.  He swung the car into the nearest vacant spot to the hospital entrance and helped Annie out.

"Are you alright?" he asked. Annie nodded, still unable to voice her fears.

"I've had a telephone call about my grandson, Kevin

Donnelly," Billy told the duty nurse at the Admissions Desk, "he's been in an accident."

The nurse turned over a page on the clipboard in front of her. "He's been admitted to the Children's Ward," she said immediately, "further down the corridor, Ward 2, it's on the right hand side."

Billy thanked her and linked Annie's arm into his. "Stay strong," he said, squeezing her hand, "Nancy needs us more than ever."

Nancy and her little family were gathered around Kevin's cot when they got to the Ward and Annie's heart almost broke as she took in how vulnerable Nancy looked.

She almost fell into her father's arms as Annie gathered Mary Anne and wee Billy into hers. "It's alright, Nancy," Billy whispered hoarsely, holding the trembling figure of his daughter, I'm here now."

Annie took Mary Anne and wee Billy out to the motor car while Billy stayed with Nancy.

"Tell me what the doctor said," Billy urged.

Nancy fixed her eyes on Kevin, willing him to open his, but he didn't move. "He says he's in a Coma," Nancy said mechanically "and they don't know if he'll............" Nancy's body began to shake again with fear and the words faded on her lips.

"Hush now," Billy said, taking her cold hands in his, "the doctors know what they're doing, Kevin will wake up soon, I'm sure." But, Billy wasn't sure if his grandson would ever be the same again. But what he was sure of was that Billy Donnelly would pay for his 'sins' and pay dearly.

"Where is he, Nancy?" Billy asked turning her to face him.

His daughter hung her head, her tears dripping onto her father's hands.

"He said he's going to enlist in the Guards again," she whispered, "and we won't be going to live at the Stannergate." Nancy looked into her father's eyes, "then he left the house and God only knows where he is now." Billy handed her a handkerchief, "dry your eyes Nancy," he said, gently, "wherever he is, I'll find him and bring him to his senses, but until then, let me and Annie look after you and the bairns."

Nancy felt a wave of panic hit her. "Kevin," she said shakily, "I can't leave Kevin here, alone!" "He won't be alone," her father said, "I'll get in touch with Isabella and she'll sit with Kevin till you get some rest."

Billy went to find a telephone to call Isabella Anderson, Annie's sister-in-law and Salvation Army stalwart. Isabella had been the one to bring Annie and Billy back together again after Euan's death and knew all about Nancy and Billy Donnelly's past.

"I'll be there in half an hour," she told Billy, when he explained about Kevin. "Thanks, Isabella," he said, "I knew I could count on you."

Before going back to the Ward, Billy asked to see the doctor who'd admitted Kevin. "I'm his Grandpa," he told Dr Morton, after he'd been ushered into a small side room, "is he going to be alright?" he asked worriedly.

Dr Morton told Billy the same as he'd told Nancy, that only time would tell if Kevin would recover and, until then, he'd be remaining in hospital under the doctor's care.

Billy nodded solemnly. "Mrs Donnelly and her family will be coming home with my wife and myself," Billy stated, "but a family friend, Mrs Anderson, will sit with Kevin in case there's any change."

The doctor nodded agreement.

They shook hands and Billy returned to the Ward where Nancy sat, unmoving, her eyes locked onto Kevin's face.

Billy felt his temper rise at the sight of his daughter's distress.

If Billy Donnelly was found to have been anywhere near Lochee......he fumed inwardly, his blood turning ice cold......he'd need more than his precious Catholic God to save him this time.

Isabella Anderson spotted Annie pacing up and down beside Billy's motor car as she came rushing through the hospital gates.

"Annie," she called, as she drew near, "I've had a telephone call from Billy to come at once, he says wee Kevin's been hurt!"

Annie hugged her sister-in-law, before moving her out of earshot of Mary Anne and wee Billy, who were sitting in the back of the motor car.

"Oh! Isabella," Annie moaned, "he's so still," she said, "and there's this big bandage on his head."

"Calm down, Annie," Isabella said softly, "wee ones recover from falls more often than not and I'm sure Kevin will be back to his old self again soon."

Annie blinked back a tear, "you think so?" she asked. Isabella nodded.

"I think so," she repeated, "now I'm going to be with him till Nancy gets some rest and I'll let you know if there's any change."

Annie took a deep breath and walked with Isabella to the entrance to the DRI. "He's in Ward 2," she said, hugging Isabella again. She had been Alex Melville's sister, but couldn't have been more different from Annie's controlling husband and the bond they'd formed when Alex had committed suicide, had sustained them both then and now.

"Chin up!" Isabella said, "God won't let Kevin down."

Annie placed her hands together and looked heavenward. He'd better not, she prayed inwardly, as Isabella disappeared through the door to the hospital.


Billy had been watching for Isabella's arrival and hurried towards her when she came into the Ward.

"Thanks for coming so quickly, Isabella," he said, holding his finger to his lips and steering her back into the corridor. "The bairn's still unconscious and Nancy's at the end of her tether."

"And where's her husband?" Isabella asked, bristling at Billy Donnelly's absence.

Billy's face tightened. "That's what I intend to find out," he said, "but until I do, Nancy and the bairns need looking after, but she won't leave Kevin on his own, so I'm asking if you'll take over for a few hours."

Isabella nodded her head, sadly, "you know I will," she said, "for as long as I'm needed."

Nancy was reluctant to leave her son, but Billy convinced her that Isabella would watch over him and that Mary Anne and wee Billy needed to be with her as well.

"I'll telephone and let you know if there's any change at all,"

Isabella assured her, "and your dad will get you back quickly in the motor car if there is."

Nancy allowed Billy to guide her out of the Ward and back to Annie at the waiting car.

Her father helped her into the back seat beside Mary Anne and wee Billy, while Annie took her place beside her husband.

"How is he?" Annie whispered.  Billy shook his head and started the engine, "time will tell," he said, "only time will tell."

# Chapter 9

Lexie had been lying down in her bedroom, mulling over the rights and wrongs of Sarah and her mother's attitude to Billy Dawson's departure from the matrimonial home and subsequent marriage to Annie, when she'd heard the telephone ringing, then Billy's muffled voice before the front door slammed, then silence.

She glanced at the clock, saw it was half past five and wondered, absently, where her mother and Billy had gone without leaving word as to when they'd be back. She went through to the kitchen and into the Pantry, finding some cheese. This would do, she decided, toasted on a slice of bread till her mother came back, but by seven o'clock, no one had appeared and Lexie began to feel anxious. It wasn't like her mother to just disappear like that. Before the war when Euan had been alive, life had been ordered and revolved around his shift pattern at Bell Street Nick.

Lexie was pondering on visiting Winnie Adams in Montrose, her friend from her early days in the WAAF, when she heard footsteps moving closer to the front door and the low murmur of voices.

"Watch that last step, Mary Anne," she heard her mother say.

"Mary Anne!" Lexie exclaimed, her brow puckering with confusion.

"What on earth......" but before she could finish asking the question, the door opened and her mother and Billy, following by Nancy and her two grown-up children, trooped in.

The expressions on all of their faces, told Lexie that all was not well.

"What's happened?" she asked her mother, as Billy ushered Nancy, Mary Anne and wee Billy into the kitchen.

"It's Kevin," she said in a whisper, "he's had an accident and he's in DRI."

"Accident!" Lexie said loudly.

"Sssshhhh!" Annie hushed her. "The doctors say he's in a Coma," she whispered, "and they're waiting for him to waken up........but I'm sure he'll be just fine," she added, with a determination she didn't feel."

Lexie felt her blood run cold. She'd seen men in the hospital at Inverness in Comas, who'd been brought back home seriously wounded, some having had to parachute from their blazing planes, but despite the best efforts of the doctors and nurses, very few of them had survived.

"Is his dad with him?" Lexie asked, anxiously, she loved King Kevin and was fully expecting Annie to say yes.

"No," she replied, grimly, "Isabella Anderson's sitting with Kevin while Nancy and her brood get some food and rest. She'll telephone us if there's any change."

"But, where is Billy then?" Lexie probed, "hasn't he been demobbed?"

Annie sighed. "Nancy doesn't know where he is, but once she and the bairns are settled, Billy will be going out to look for him."

"I'll go with him," Lexie volunteered, instantly, "he'll need an extra pair of eyes on the lookout, especially if he's driving."

Annie hugged her daughter. "Thanks Lexie," she whispered, "that'll be a great help."

Lexie pulled on her coat and hat, glad to feel of some use and followed Annie into the kitchen. Nancy was nervously picking at the button holes of her coat while Mary Anne and wee Billy watched her, guilt and fear robbing them of their usual chattering.

Annie bustled over to the stove and picked up the kettle. "I'll look after things here," she murmured into Billy's ear, "please find him as soon as you can and get him back to Nancy."

Billy nodded mechanically, his mind elsewhere, "I'll find him," he said, quietly "and when I do......."

Annie grabbed his sleeve, fully aware of the animosity the young man had aroused in her husband, "please Billy," she begged, "just bring him back."

Lexie's voice interrupted the moment, now aware of Billy's anger. "I'll go with you," she said firmly, "keep an eye out for him as you drive."

Billy nodded and pushed back his chair, the sound of Lexie's determined voice taking the edge of his temper.

She leant over Nancy's shoulder, kissing the top of her cousin's head.

"We'll find him," she said, "and King Kevin will be fine," she added, "people come out of Coma's all the time, especially children," she said, the white lie slipping too easily from her lips.

Billy was already out of the kitchen and Lexie hurried after him.

"Have you any idea where he is?" she asked, breathing in short gasps as she ran down the stairs after him and out of the close into Albert Street.

Billy unlocked the motor and helped Lexie into the passenger seat.

"I know exactly where he is," he said, his eyes cold and menacing,

"Herons Lane in Lochee." Lexie didn't understand but knew not to ask further.

The drive to Lochee was long and uncomfortable as Billy's motor car bumped and jolted over the cassies and tramlines.

"Why are you so sure you'll find him in Lochee?" Lexie asked, loudly, over the noise of the car's engine.

Billy gripped the steering wheel tighter, "because that's where the prostitute lives," he said through gritted teeth, "that's why I'm sure."

The rest of the drive was taken in silence.

Gladys Kelly was curled up into Billy Donnelly's chest, her eyes closed and her heart beating softly. As usual, Billy had fallen into a deep slumber, his body and mind sated with Gladys's lovemaking. She never failed to arouse him nor failed to satisfy him and now that he was back in her bed, all her dreams and longings for him, unbelievably, had come true.

"Billy," she whispered into his chest, "I love you." There, she'd said it, he didn't hear it, of course, he was dead to the world, but it felt good to say it just the same as Gladys Kelly too, fell asleep.

The banging on the door was so loud, both Billy and Gladys were instantly awake and alert. "Who the Hell's that?" Billy asked, jumping out of the bed and pulling on his trousers.

"I'm not expecting anyone," Gladys told him weakly, grabbing her skirt from the bedside chair and holding it against her nakedness.

"OPEN UP."

Billy felt sick as he realised who was on the other side of the door, but there was no escape, he thrust his shirt over his head and opened the door.

"BASTARD," Billy shouted grabbing his son-in-law round the throat, "FILTHY BASTARD."

Gladys melted into the furthest corner of the room while Lexie tried to pull Billy away.

"STOP IT," she shouted, hysterically fearing that Billy Donnelly was going to be murdered in front of her.

"REMEMBER NANCY AND THE BAIRNS," she screamed, "REMEMBER KEVIN."

The words seemed to penetrate through the red mist of anger that was surrounding Billy Dawson and he loosened his grip.

His son-in-law fell to the floor, gasping for breath, while Gladys Kelly sought refuge under the kitchen table. She knew Billy Dawson of old, when he'd forced her to move to Lochee and out of the reach of Billy Donnelly and his lust for her.

"GET UP," Billy ordered, icily "and make yourself decent," while Lexie clung to his arm, dreading what would happen if she let go.

As soon as Billy was clothed, his father-in-law pushed him roughly through the door before turning his attention to Gladys Kelly.

Lexie didn't know what he said to the woman, but her eyes grew wide with fear as he spoke to her naked form. He guided Lexie out of the door and slammed it shut behind him. Billy Donnelly was leaning heavily against the motor, unable to understand how Billy Dawson had found him.   Billy swung him round to face him.  With an almighty slap he spun him off his feet before pushing him into the back of the motor and wordlessly, heading to the Infirmary and his grandson.

# Chapter 10

The patients had been bedded down for the night and the ward lights dimmed when the trio arrived at the Infirmary.

"Why are we here?" Billy Donnelly asked, nervously, panic beginning to form in the pit of his stomach.

"Wait in the car" Billy said to Lexie, his voice dangerously flat, "we won't be long."

He opened the back door of the car and waited while Billy scrambled out.

"Why are we at the Infirmary," he asked again, his eyes wide as Billy gripped his arm and steered him towards the entrance.

Their footsteps echoing on the hard, stone corridor, they made their way to Ward 2. Noises of snuffling and whimpering came to Billy Donnelly's ears and he stopped walking forwards.

"Are there bairns in there?" he gulped as he tried to peer through the gloom.

Billy shoved him onwards. "Take a look for yourself," he said....."unless your eyes have been blinded by your lust."

Billy flinched and inched further into the Ward, his legs seeming to have lost their ability to move. He screwed his eyes up as the shape of a woman sitting beside a cot took form.

"Is that Isabella Anderson?" Billy asked, moving towards the woman.

Billy Dawson watched as his son-in-law looked into the cot before falling on his knees at the sight of his son's motionless body. Silently, Isabella stood up and came towards Billy.

"Where was he?" she asked simply.

Billy shook his head but didn't answer. "Is there any change?" he asked.

Isabella shook her head. "The nurses have been checking him every hour, but so far, he hasn't stirred."

Billy sighed deeply. "Pray for him, Isabella," he said, "and for Nancy and her young 'uns."

They both looked on as Billy Donnelly wept beside his son's cot.

"C'mon," he said to Isabella, "I'll take you home and tomorrow......I'll deal with Mr Donnelly."

Lexie was pacing anxiously when she saw Billy and Isabella coming towards her. She hurried to meet them.

"He's with his son," Billy said, before Lexie could ask him anything "and we're going home."

It was almost midnight before Billy and Lexie got back to Albert Street.

Annie was waiting, her mind racing along confused roads and dead ends. She'd managed to get Nancy and her two youngsters to try to get some sleep, using Ian's old room as a makeshift dormitory, while she sat by the telephone, praying for good news.

"Did you find him?" she asked nervously as soon as Billy and Lexie came through the door.

"We found him," Lexie said clenching her fists as she relived the awfulness of their visit to Herons Lane and Gladys Kelly.

"Was he with her?" Nancy's trembling voice suddenly cut through the dimness of the lobby.

Quickly, Billy stepped towards her and wrapped his arm around her shoulders. "He's with Kevin," he told her, "and tomorrow, we'll sort things out."

"Kevin," Nancy whimpered, "is he awake yet?"

"Not yet," Lexie whispered, "but he'll be fine," she added, "he'll wake up soon." Again, the lie came easily. Lexie's time as a WAAF had needed her to lie time and again, to hide the truth of impending death from worried families. And here she was, the war over, doing the same thing to Nancy, knowing there was nothing anyone could do, but wait till Kevin's little body came back to them or drifted deeper into unconsciousness and death.

Annie guided Nancy back into the bedroom. "Try to get some sleep, Nancy," she said quietly, "Your dad will fix things tomorrow and everything will be fine."

But Nancy didn't get any sleep that night and the next day her eyes were hollow and dark circles were etched below her lashes, as she dragged

herself into the early morning coldness of the room.

No one had slept much, but Billy was prepared for his next encounter with his son-in-law by the time the clock had struck six.

"Make sure Nancy  eats something," Billy instructed Annie "and keep them all here till I get back."

Annie helped him on with his overcoat and kissed his cheek.

"Be careful," she said, knowing his temper where Billy Donnelly was concerned.

Billy nodded.  "I'll be careful," he said, "and keep by the telephone incase there's news."

His son-in-law was where Billy had left him the night before. He hoped he was suffering the way Nancy was, as he approached Kevin's cot.

"Any change?" Billy asked, coldly.

Billy Donnelly shook his head, his drooping shoulders and red eyes telling their story.  Kevin was slipping deeper into unconsciousness and no one seemed able to do anything to stop it.

"Get up," Billy said, "the motor's outside and waiting."

"Where are we going?" the young man asked, confusion filling his soul.

"Somewhere where you can't do any more damage to Nancy nor the rest of her family."

Billy's eyes widened, he'd had a beating from Billy Dawson before and knew what he was capable of, but this felt different and soldier or not, he was suddenly very afraid of his father-in-law. He pulled himself up from the chair and faced the ice-cold wrath of Billy Dawson.

"The motor," Billy repeated, nodding towards the door.

"I'm so sorry," his son-in-law murmured, again and again, as he dragged his guilt across the linoleum floor of the Ward.

The Ward Sister appeared at Billy's side.

"He hasn't left the bairn's side all night," she told Billy indicating the departing figure.

"What are the doctors saying about the bairn?" Billy asked, ignoring her comment.

The Sister looked gently at the sleeping child, then at his Grandad and shook her head. "Only God knows if he'll recover," she said, placing a comforting hand on Billy's arm. "Don't give up hope," she added softly, before quietly going back to her duties.

Billy pulled up the chair and leant over the cot. His grandson's life had barely begun and now....... He felt tears begin to form in his eyes and for the first time since he'd come back from fighting in 'the war to end all wars,' shell-shocked and almost broken, he began to pray.

In the silence of the early morning, the world seemed to be standing still as the old man pleaded for the life of his grandson. Holding Kevin's tiny hand in his, he repeated the simple words. "God, save my wee laddie, save King Kevin."

It could have been minutes it could have been hours, as Billy sat praying beside the cot, gazing through his tears at his grandson, when suddenly, there was the whisper of movement in the bairn's eyelids.

Billy blinked and leant closer. "Kevin," he murmured, "it's Grandad..... can you hear me? I've come to take you home."

The eye movement increased and Kevin's tiny chest seemed to take in a deep breath of life-giving air. Billy felt a surge of joy course through him. King Kevin was coming back to life.

"Sister?" he called out, "Sister, come quick, the bairn's waking up."

The Sister, followed by the Duty Doctor, hurried towards Kevin's cot.

The Doctor, immediately, listened to Kevin's heart with his Stethoscope and felt for his pulse. The smile on the nurse's face said it all as the Doctor nodded towards her.

"I think you're right, Mr Dawson" he said, "the child is coming back to us." He took Billy's hand and shook it. "This is what we've been waiting for," he said smiling broadly, "now I'll ask you, please, to leave things to us to make sure he fully comes round." He indicated to the Sister to bring the screen round the cot.

Billy shook his head in disbelief. "God heard me" he said, his eyes meeting those of the nurse, that were brimming with tears. Smiling, knowingly, the Sister guided Billy to the Duty Desk and the telephone.

"I think mum might want to hear the good news," she said, "and I'll get a nurse to bring you a nice cup of tea."

Billy gazed at the telephone, still stunned at his prayers being answered. Shakily, he dialled his number. Annie picked up the telephone on the first ring.

"It's me," he said, simply, "Kevin's woken up!"

He heard Annie's voice calling out to Nancy. "Kevin's woken up," she shouted excitedly, "come quickly."

Nancy's trembling voice came to his ear down the telephone line. "Dad?" she said, fearfully, "is it true?"

"It's true," Billy assured her, "he's awake."

Nancy almost dropped the receiver as she handed it back to Annie.

"He's woken up," she said, barely able to get the words out.

Annie held her hand tightly as Billy's voice sounded again.

"I'll come and get you all soon," he said, "and you can see Kevin for yourselves."

Everything was going to be alright, he told himself, as he hung up the receiver and rubbed the tension from his face.

Then he remembered Kevin's father, waiting for him and the punishment he would bring him.

Billy slowly drank the tea the nurse had brought him, but the hatred for his son-in-law that he had brought with him to the hospital had, somehow, evaporated. There was a God, he now knew for certain, Kevin was proof of that and knowing this, seemed to have calmed his very soul.

'Vengeance is mine, said the Lord,' Billy heard himself quote, as he remembered the words from the Bible. He thanked the Sister and made his way outside, where Nancy's husband waited.

Billy Donnelly was gazing at the city spread out before him. The smoke from the mill chimneys hung in the sky and mixed with the smoke from the coal fires of the mill workers homes, adding to the murkiness of the dreich Scottish morning.

Cox's stack towered above all else and Billy's mind went back to his younger days working at the mill and first falling in love with Nancy. He would have died for her then, but right now, he just wanted to die for the pity of it all.

Everything he had hoped for when he and Nancy were wed and Mary Anne had been born, had crumbled to nothing and all because of his lust for Gladys Kelly. He kicked a stone away with the toe of his boot, whatever Billy Dawson had in store for him, he deserved and he knew it.

"He's awake," he heard the deep voice of his father-in-law say, "Kevin's woken up."

Billy could hardly believe his ears. He swung round to face the man who hated him.

His body shook from head to toe as he reached out to clutch Billy's coat.

"Are you sure?" he managed to stammer, "Kevin's going to be alright?"

"Get in the motor," was all Billy said, "Nancy needs you."

—-—oOo—-—

# Chapter 11

The news that Kevin was out of his Coma, filled the room with new hope.

"Your dad will be here soon," Annie said to Nancy, regaining her energy and allowing herself to smile again.  She hugged Mary Anne and wee Billy and ushered them into the kitchen, leaving Lexie and Nancy in the sitting room.

Lexie was still reverberating in disgust from the sight of Billy Donnelly with the naked Gladys Kelly and her heart went out to Nancy, who remained despondent, despite the good news about Kevin. How could she bear to be near the man, Lexie wondered, whose need for the prostitute was almost obsessive, while the love for his family seemed all but gone?

"Is there anything I can do?" Lexie asked into the silence.

A faint smile crossed Nancy's lips.  "There's nothing anyone can do," she replied, almost to herself, "what's done is done and can't be undone." Lexie felt powerless to help.

"Your dad will be here soon," she said, trying to bring some lightness into the gloom, "I'm sure he'll make everything alright again."

The sound of the front door opening and closing met Lexie's ears.

Quickly, she stood up, "there," she said, "that'll be him now."

But Billy wasn't alone.  The tall, dishevelled frame of Billy Donnelly came into the room.  "Kevin's going to be alright, Nancy," he said nervously, his eyes seeking reassurance from his wife that she was glad to see him.

Nancy stood and smoothed her skirt. "Can you leave us alone please, Lexie," she said, quietly, "tell dad I'll be with him shortly."

A strange calmness seemed to surround Nancy, as her husband inched further into the room. Lexie nodded and made for the door, whatever it was that Nancy needed to say to Billy was for his ears only.

As soon as Lexie had gone, Billy moved towards his wife, "I'm sorry Nancy," he began, "I didn't know Kevin was hurt....I was at the Thrums and got a bit drunk......" but Nancy stopped him in his tracks.

"I know where you were," she said icily, "so don't try to tell me any more of your lies. Billy cursed inwardly. His father-in-law, he realised, panicking, must have told her where he'd been found. But he'd always talked Nancy round in the past and this time, he assured himself, might be a bit more of a problem, but she'd believe him, eventually, just like she'd always done.

"I was in the Thrums!" he exclaimed, raising his shoulders and opening his arms, in disbelief, "I got drunk and can't remember any more, that's............"

"LIAR!" Nancy shouted. Billy shut his mouth. "GO BACK TO YOUR WHORE," she spat, the words fierce and brooking no argument. "AND DON'T COME BACK...THIS SHAM OF A MARRIAGE IS OVER!"

The shouting had brought Billy Dawson from the kitchen. He opened the door of the sitting room and heard the last three words.....'MARRIAGE IS OVER.' Without hesitation, he put his hand, firmly, on Billy's shoulder.

"You heard," he said, steering his son-in-law out into the lobby.

Billy opened the door and pushed the young man out with a warning. "The next time we meet," he said, bluntly, "it had better be at your funeral."

When her father returned to the sitting room Nancy had dissolved into a sea of tears.

"It's alright," Billy soothed, "everything will be alright now."

He held his daughter till the tears of grief and fear subsided. These would be the last tears she shed, he vowed. Life for his daughter and her family would be as happy as he could make it and as for Billy Donnelly, well, if God answered his prayers again, he would rot in Hell.

"Come in," Billy said in response to the gentle knocking at the sitting room door.

Annie's concerned face looked into the room. Nancy was leaning against her father, exhausted and tear-stained. "Is she alright?" she mouthed to Billy. Billy nodded, "she will be," he said, tightening his grip on Nancy's shoulder and turning her to face him.

"Time to go and see Kevin," he said, gently, "get him well again and ready to come home."

"Home?" Nancy echoed, tears threatening to fall again. "Yes, HOME," Billy emphasised, "but not to that miserable flat in Victoria Road, nor to that husband of yours," he told her, firmly. Annie didn't understand, where were Nancy and her family going and without her husband?"

"Lexie, Mary Anne and wee Billy crowded into the sitting room, wondering where everyone had gone. Nancy seemed to get her second wind at the sight of her offspring.

"Kevin's going to be fine," she said, standing up and smoothing her hair into place, "so let's go and see him for ourselves," she nodded towards her father, "grandpa is going to take us to the hospital in his motor car so let's have no more sadness," she told the two worried faces gazing at her for assurance.

The strain of the last few days begun to visibly ebb and Billy gave Nancy a fatherly hug before ushering everyone out into the lobby to get their coats.

"Is dad with Kevin," wee Billy asked his mother in a whisper, as they made their way to the motor car? He loved his father dearly and was becoming more and more concerned at his disappearance.

Nancy held a finger to her lips to hush him. The time to speak about Billy Donnelly wasn't now and it was a conversation that Nancy was

dreading, but one that would have to take place. The marriage was over and there would be no going back.

Kevin was sitting up in his cot when the little party arrived. Nancy hurried toward him, followed hard on her heels by Mary Anne and wee Billy.

"Look," she cried to her youngsters, "Kevin's fine again, just fine."

She bent down and kissed the bairn on the top of his head while Lexie, Billy and Annie watched, relief washing over them all.

"Where's Billy?" Annie asked, the last time she'd seen him was at her home when he'd gone to speak to Nancy in the sitting room.

Lexie avoided eye contact with her mother and Billy Dawson tightened his lips. "Not now, Annie," he said, "suffice to say, he won't be causing Nancy any more hurt.

Annie drew back. "What do you mean?"

Billy steered her out into the corridor. "She's told him the marriage is over," he said, "and as far as I'm concerned, he could be dead." Annie's hand flew to her mouth in shock. "But, Billy........." she tried to say that he was the bairns' father, but her husband was having none of it.

"Don't go feeling sorry for him," he admonished Annie, "he's probably scuttled back to that prostitute, like a rat down a hole and that's the best place for him."

Annie fell silent. Too much was happening and she needed time to understand it all. She'd speak to Lexie when she had the chance, maybe she understood Nancy's situation better, but her fears for her niece and the bairns were increasing. With no man to support her, they were in serious trouble.

When Billy Donnelly finally made it back to Gladys Kelly's hovel, he was frozen stiff and devoid of any emotion. Usually, when he visited Gladys he was hot and greedy for her services, but this time, he was just desperate. If she didn't take him in, he would probably die on the streets of cold and hunger.

His son was going to be alright, he repeated to himself, but his marriage was well and truly over and if Billy Dawson had anything to do with it, he's never see Nancy or the bairns again.

Gladys's door creaked open at his knock, her face, white with fear and shock looked around the gap.

"Let me in," Billy urged, shaking with cold. Gladys hesitated.

"Please?" he begged.

The door opened and he hurried inside, making for the weak fire that was smouldering in the grate.

Wordlessly, she handed him a glass and a half-empty bottle of Port.

Billy took them and poured himself a measure of the sweet liquid. He could feel it burn his throat and heat his innards.

"Thanks," he said, refilling the glass. "You always did know how to treat a man." Unlike his wife, he wanted to add, but didn't. He'd have to tread carefully, or this last refuge might also be lost, he realised, pushing the bottle over towards Gladys.

"I've left her," Billy announced bluntly, draining his glass.

Gladys frowned. She knew he was lying, after the visit from Billy Dawson, Gladys was under no illusion that Nancy didn't know where he'd been found. She wished it was true, but instinct told her that Billy Donnelly was only back at her door because he'd been thrown out by his wife.

There was a time when she would have given everything to hear those words, but now, as she looked at his gaunt face and sunken eyes, she knew for certain that Billy Donnelly would never be hers.

"Whaur will you go now?" she asked. He turned started eyes towards her.

"I thought you and me......"

Gladys shook her head. "I've a business to run," she said, looking around the dingy room and pouring herself the last of the Port "and I dinna mix business wi' pleasure."

Billy flinched, his hand trembling as he reached out to take her arm.

Gladys pulled back, sure now that his only reason for being there was desperation.

Billy hadn't expected this! "I don't understand," he spluttered, pulling his chair around till he was next to her. "I've left her," he emphasised, "I've left Nancy and the bairns to be with you."

Gladys met his desperate gaze. "Na you've no'," she said, her heart not believing what her voice was saying, "you only want a bed for the nicht, till you can get back wi' your wife."

Billy squeezed her hand. "Gladys, Gladys," he implored her, "you've got it all wrong, I've left her because I..........I love you!"

The words hung in the air. Billy repeated them, this time, more firmly. Somehow he had to convince Gladys he loved her, or the future for him would be on the streets. With no job, very little money and nowhere to live, Gladys was his only option........at the moment.

His eyes never left her face. "Gladys," he whispered, "you know it's always been you." He saw her begin to weaken and pushed home his advantage. "Please, believe me........I love you."

Gladys felt tears well in her eyes. She'd waited so long for Billy Donnelly to love her, like he loved Nancy and now.........he was here and the reason for his being with her didn't matter. He was here.

"Div you mean it?" she asked, her insides shaking, "really mean it."

Billy had won and he knew it. "Of course I mean it," he assured her, putting his arm around her and pulling her towards him. He was safe for now and tomorrow would take care of itself.

"Let's go to bed," he said, relief flooding his system "and I'll show you how much I love you."

Gladys nodded, her heart longing for him but her head was doubtful.

"If yir lying to me," she began, but Billy stopped her saying anything more with a kiss.

"Trust me," he murmured "I love you."

# Chapter 12

Lexie gazed at the ceiling of her bedroom.  The house was quiet now, everyone finally bedded down for the night.  As usual, Nancy had managed to 'land on her feet', Lexie mused, despite being almost as guilty as her husband of adultery, but with Jim Murphy.  She remembered seeing them both 'smooching' at the Palais and was in no doubt Nancy would have taken him in permanently, if his wife hadn't found out.

Until Kevin was born, everyone had doubts about who the bairn's father was, but once he arrived it was plain that Billy was his dad and the marriage seemed to get patched up, with the help of Billy Dawson, until now that is, now it seemed to be over for good.

A feeling of helplessness crept into Lexie's soul. Despite a world war, her experiences in the WAAF and her own short-lived marriage to Robbie Robertson, it felt as if nothing had changed!  Here she was, back in her childhood bedroom, her mother still baking and fussing over her and Nancy still being 'rescued' by her dad from problems, Lexie felt sure, were mostly of her own making.

Eventually, she fell into a fitful sleep, but soon woke up, barely rested and too early.

She clicked on the bedside light, pushed back the bedcovers and sat up. Facing her on the dressing table was a photograph of Lexie and her brother Ian.  She remembered the photo being taken by a street photographer who was snapping people as they walked towards him in the Murraygate.  Ian too had survived the war and was living with his girlfriend's family in Carlisle and soon to be married, if his short letters were anything to go by.

Lexie smiled to herself. "I hope you get better luck than me," she whispered to the photo, her mind racing back to her wedding to Robbie on board the Destroyer. Two months later, he'd been torpedoed at sea and killed.

Lexie shook away the tears and returned the photo to the dresser. She looked at her watch, nearly six o'clock. Her mother would be getting up soon to start breakfast for Nancy and her brood, Billy would be organising their next visit to the Infirmary and Lexie would be expected to join them and......................she felt herself begin to panic. This wasn't what she wanted. She wanted her freedom back, get away from Dundee and back into the wide world, not to become her old self again! She'd seen what was happening to Sarah Dawson, living with her bitter mother till she died and she could escape.

She couldn't face breakfast with them all, chattering and smiling.

Quickly, she pulled on some clothes and without a backward glance, she slipped out of the slumbering house and into the dark Winter morning.

Shivering, she pulled the collar of her coat up around her ears and was glad she'd left her gloves in the coat pockets. Lexie's shoes clipped along the pavement as she made her way down Albert Street towards the town centre. She didn't know where she was going, just that she had to be going somewhere and as far away from her fears as possible.

By the time she'd walked as far as King Street, her mind was steadying. Baxters Mill loomed out of the dimness of the street lights and she quickly crossed the road, fearing its nearness would somehow draw her in.

The small shops were already lit up as the owners prepared their produce for opening time and Lexie found herself staring into the window of Harry Duncan's butcher shop. She was fifteen again and madly in love with the butcher's boy, Robbie Robertson. He'd given her a ring to prove his love, but Lexie had been frightened by his intensity and had run away from him. How she wished now that she hadn't. Robbie had joined the

Merchant Navy then and it was that decision, all those years earlier that had resulted in his untimely death at sea.

She was brought back to reality by the sound of the shop door being unlocked and Harry Duncan's grizzled head peering out at her.

"Lexie!" he exclaimed. "It is Lexie isn't it?" Lexie nodded.

"Come away in lassie," he said, anxiously, "whut are yi' doin' out in this weather and at this time o' the moarnin'.?"

Lexie could only shrug. She didn't know why she was there.

"Come on through tae the back," Harry Duncan said, kindly, "the kettle's just boiled an' eh wiz jist aboot to hae a cuppa ma'self."

He steered Lexie towards an old basket chair with a worn cushion covering its creaking weave. Lexie sunk into the chair and watched as Harry poured the tea into two chipped cups and handed her one.

He knew all about the death of Robbie. The street had been buzzing with the talk of his bravery and how his widow had only been married to him for weeks before he'd been killed. He also knew that the widow was Lexie. Her mother had told him the bad news when it happened.

"You look tired, lassie," he said, "but eh'm jist glad tae see yi' back, safe and well."

Harry's kindness was too much and tears began to flow down Lexie's cheeks. Her life was a mess. All her plans for the future with Robbie as his wife were now gone and the end of the war meant she couldn't even stay in the WAAF.

"I'm not glad I'm back," she sniffed, as the tears began to subside."

Harry's eyes narrowed in concern. "Too many mem'ries?" he asked.

Lexie's eyes met his. "I have to get away," she said, solemnly, "with Robbie gone, there's nothing for me here and I'm not going back there," she added, a determination coming into her voice as she indicated Baxters Mill.

Harry nodded sagely. He'd seen Lexie grow from a young girl into womanhood and had been delighted when he'd heard about her wedding to Robbie. But now, she was his widow and seemed, to Harry, like that little girl again.  Lost and scared.

The old butcher leaned towards her.  "If you tak' my advice," he said, "you'll dae whut you did when you merried Robbie......follae yir heart."

Lexie's blue eyes held onto the words.  Was it really so simple?

The fates seemed to be conspiring to force her back into the past and the future seemed so uncertain and unsafe, she felt almost frozen in time, unable to see a way out.

"Well?"  Harry's voice cut into her thoughts, "whut's it to be," he asked, "whut's yir heart saying Lexie?"

"My heart's saying I don't want to stay in Dundee, but my head's telling me I don't have a choice."

Harry smiled.  "There's aye a choice, lassie," he said, "jist dinna mak' the mistake o' lettin' ithers mak' yir mind up for you."

Lexie felt a small ball of hope form in her chest.  Harry Duncan was right. Her heart was telling her to leave Dundee and that's what she must do, how she was going to do this was another matter, but making the decision to go, already felt right.

"Thanks Harry," she said, stretching out her hand to shake his, "for the tea and for the advice."

Harry shook her hand warmly.  "Ony time lassie," he said, escorting her to the shop door. "Whaurever yi' go," he added, unlocking the door for her, "dinna forget auld Dundee an' its folk, 'cause we winna forget you."

King Street was already beginning to waken up as Harry Duncan's door closed behind her.  She watched as the Mill workers, heads bent against the cold and booted feet clanging over the tram lines, hurried through the loading bay doors towards the Weaving Flats. Lexie shuddered, there was no place for her at Baxters anymore, she now knew for sure. Her heart was turning her away from the past and she was now determined to listen to it.

She hurried down King Street and found herself heading towards the Seagate and the bus station.  In a flash, she knew where her next step would be.  She would go to Montrose and see Winnie Adams. Winnie would understand how she felt. They'd kept in touch since that first day when they'd met on the train going to the RAF Camp at Wilmslow in England and their new lives as WAAF's.  Lexie smiled at the memory as she entered the bus station, her heart already telling her she was going in the right direction.

A sleepy-headed ticket clerk peered through his window at Lexie then at the clock. "Whaur tae?" he asked.

"Montrose," Lexie said.

The clerk checked his timetables. "There's a bus gaein' tae Aiberdeen," he told her, "stoppin' at ah toons on the way and that includes Montrose."

Lexie nodded enthusiastically, "what time does it leave?"

The clerk looked at the clock again.  "Now!"  He pointed to the row of buses, one of which was lit up with the engine running.

Lexie flew out of the door and onto the bus, flopping down in a front seat.  "Perfect timing," she said quietly, Nancy and her brood, Billy Dawson and her mother forgotten, the fates were back on her side.

The Bluebird bus backed out of the station and the peroxide blonde 'Clippie' issued Lexie with her ticket.

"You're oot an' aboot early," she smiled, "or jist goin' hame maybee?" she added winking, knowingly.

Lexie laughed.  "Just an early bird," she said, slipping her ticket into her purse while the conductress moved onto the other passengers.

The sky was lightening now and Lexie felt her heart beat faster as the bus trundled out of the bus station and onto Broughty Ferry Road and Montrose.

Winnie's parents house overlooked the Montrose Basin and, right now, the tide was out and the mud was studded with gulls and waders, searching for worms and open shells.

Lexie alighted from the bus and, for the first time, realised it was still early in the day and wondered if the household would be up and about, never mind open to visitors.

She needn't have worried, the door was opened by one of Winnie's brothers. "It's for you," he shouted over his shoulder without asking Lexie's name and she could hear her friend's voice calling from inside the kitchen. "I'll be there in a minute."

Winnie hurried to the door, struggling into her coat and with a slice of toast tangling from her lips. The toast promptly fell when she saw who was at the door.

" LEXIE!" she exclaimed, throwing her arms around her, "I don't' believe it." Lexie hugged Winnie back and was soon hustled into the warmth of the kitchen. "I thought you were someone from the Base!" she gushed.

"It's Lexie Melville," Winnie announced to her bemused parents, grinning widely, "the WAAF from Dundee."

Bemused, everyone nodded and smiled a welcome.

"You'll be late for your work if you don't hurry," Winnie's father said to her. She turned to Lexie. "I'm workin' now as a civvy," she said breathlessly, "but I'll be back at dinner-time, so don't disappear before then."

Lexie assured her she'd wait as Winnie rushed out of the door, calling after her to her mother to feed their visitor.

Winnie's two brothers followed suit and headed off to work, leaving Lexie and Mr and Mrs Adams in the sudden stillness.

"Have you eaten?" Mrs Adams asked Lexie.

Lexie shook her head, the smell of bacon awakening her tastebuds.

"We'll soon sort that," she said, turning to the black range and the frying pan.

"So, you're a WAAF are you?" the deep voice of Jock Adams asked Lexie.

"Not any longer," Lexie replied, "I've been demobbed same as Winnie, and need to find work.

"So, you're thinkin' o' joinin' our Winnie at the base?" he asked.

Lexie frowned in confusion. "She's working at RAF Montrose?" Lexie queried, "but she's been demobbed too, hasn't she?"

"Aye, she has that," he told her, "but she's workin' as a civilian worker, or civvy as she calls herself."

Lexie couldn't believe what she was hearing. Was it possible that she too could go back to Lossiemouth, this time to work as a civilian?

She needed answers, but they'd have to wait until Winnie came back at dinner-time.

A plate of fried bacon and scrambled eggs was placed before Lexie.

"There's plenty o' tea in the pot," Bertha Adams said, turning the handle of the teapot towards Lexie, "so eat up lassie, you look like you could do with a feed."

There was a way out, Lexie told herself, excitedly, she didn't have to stay in Dundee if she didn't want too, she could return to Lossiemouth and live again!

Lexie tucked into the most wonderful breakfast she had ever eaten, much to the amusement of Jock and Bertha Adams. For the first time since her demob, Lexie knew where she was going.

—·—oOo—·—

# Chapter 13

Annie didn't realise that Lexie had gone 'till after everyone had left for the hospital.  She knocked lightly on her daughter's bedroom door and called her name.

"Lexie, are you awake?"

Getting no answer, Annie eased the door open and looked in. Lexie's unmade bed was there, but she wasn't in it.

Unable to understand where her daughter could have gone so early, Annie felt a slight unease at the sight of Lexie's empty room.  She'd just got her back now the war was over and she was looking forward to mothering her again.  She'd missed Lexie since she'd enlisted in the WAAF and just wanted things to be as they were, before the war had taken her daughter from her, but unknown to Annie, Lexie had other ideas for her future.

Lexie spent the morning being regaled with tales of Winnie when she was a wee girl and how proud her parents were of her helping to 'win the war.' Winnie's return for her dinner was heralded by a rush of cold air as she breezed into the kitchen, her smile stretching from ear to ear.

"We need to catch up," she said, briskly, taking hold of Lexie's hand and pulling her up from the chair, "we'll get something to eat at the Base," she called over her shoulder, ushering Lexie towards the door as she spoke.

Jock and Bertha Adams were lost for words as the two girls hurried from the kitchen.  "Well!" Bertha sighed, turning the gas off under the pot of Stovies, "she'll just have to have her dinner at tea-time."  Jock nodded in agreement, "as long as they're eaten then" he said, his frugal nature asserting itself. He lit his pipe and watched as his wife began clearing the kitchen table and boiling a kettle of water for the dish washing.

"Women," he muttered in bemusement, blowing the tobacco smoke into air and secretly glad he was the man of the house.

Breathlessly, Lexie hurried after Winnie. "Slow down," she gasped, "where's the fire?"

Winnie gave her a knowing look. "No fire," she quipped, "but there's someone who wants to meet you and I think you might want to meet him too."

Lexie shrugged her shoulders in acceptance. She didn't know anyone at RAF Montrose, but Winnie just winked and pointed towards the perimeter fence in the distance.

The airmen on duty at the gate nodded their arrival with a smile at Winnie and a questioning eye at Lexie, but after a whispered conversation with Winnie, they waved them through.

The familiarity of the Base brought a lump to Lexie's throat. Everything was in order and the personnel, some in uniform and some, like Winnie dressed in civilian clothing, went about their business with purpose and briskness.

Lexie took a deep breath as a feeling of 'coming home' crept into her heart and she knew now, for certain, that this was where her future lay.

Winnie pointed to one of the Hangers. "In there," she whispered, "is an old friend of yours and he's looking forward to seeing you again."

Lexie became more confused. "But........." Winnie hushed her and nodded towards the Hanger.

Lexie made her way to the open Hanger and looked into the dim interior. There was only one person inside, hunched over a desk and writing up some paperwork. Whoever wanted to see her must have left. She approached the figure at the desk, her eyes becoming accustomed to the gloom as she did so. "Excuse me," she said, "I believe I'm expected, but I don't know......."

The handsome face of Sgt Brady looked up at her, "remember me?" he asked, standing up and grinning.

Lexie's mouth fell open in disbelief. Sgt Brady, her NCO from RAF Lossiemouth was right in front of her, even more handsome than ever in his civilian clothes.

"And it's Terry Brady," he said, "not a sergeant anymore."

The sound of someone clearing their throat, made Lexie turn towards the door.  "Can I come in?" Winnie asked with a grin.

Terry signalled her towards them.  "Let's go to the NAAFI," he said, "I think Lexie could do with a cuppa."

Once they were settled at a table with their tea, the noise of the other diners faded into the distance as Terry Brady and Winnie told Lexie about working as a civilian at the RAF Base now the war was over and Lexie's skills would be more than welcomed, just like theirs had been.

Lexie could hardly believe what they were saying, but as the hour wore on, her way forward became more and more obvious.

As soon as she got back to Dundee, she would write to Wing Commander Johnny Johnson at RAF Lossiemouth and offer her services as a civilian.

The rest of the day passed in a blur with the promise of a return visit to Montrose and a hug from Winnie as she waved Lexie goodbye as she boarded the bus back home.

It was early evening when Lexie finally made it back to Dundee and Albert Street, where Billy Dawson and her anxious mother were awaiting her arrival.

"You don't think anything's happened to her, do you?" Annie asked.

Billy glanced at the clock, "it's barely 8 o'clock," he said "and she's a big girl now, Annie, well able to look after herself."  But never the less the sound of the front door opening made Annie jump up and run to meet Lexie in the lobby.

"Where have you been?" she asked her daughter, anxiously, you've been gone all day and we didn't know…….."

The sound of Billy clearing his throat stopped Annie's rush of words.

"I think Lexie needs a cup of tea and one of your scones," he told Annie quietly, as he ushered Lexie into the front room.

"Your mum's been a bit worried about you, that's all," Billy said, "you know what she's like," he added, before lighting up a cigarette and indicating for Lexie to sit on the sofa.

She looked around the room for signs of Nancy and her brood, but there were none.

"Where's Nancy?" she asked.

"Gone back to Victoria Road......for now, that is."

The door opened and Annie came in bearing a full tray of tea things and scones.

"There," she said with satisfaction, "I imagine you're starving," she smiled to Lexie, "having been out all day."

Lexie grimaced. She realised that her mother was never going to stop treating her like a child and her determination to write to Johnny Johnson was reinforced. But, before she could say anything about her decision to return to Lossiemouth, Billy spoke.

"Now Annie," Billy began, "let Lexie have her tea before we tell her about everything."

Lexie's frown deepened. "I'm not hungry, actually," she said, a knot of tension forming in her stomach. "Tell me what?"

Billy stubbed his cigarette out and took a deep breath.

"As you know, Nancy's gone back to Victoria Road," he began, "but Billy Donnelly won't be joining her."

Lexie nodded, "Is the separation final then?" she asked.

"It is," he told her, before continuing.

"She'll be moving to a place at the Stannergate I've found to rent for the four of them, but if she's to manage to keep it, she'll have to find work."

Lexie was getting confused, what was this to do with her.

She was soon to find out.

"So, it's like this Lexie," he said slowly, "Billy was going to be coming to work at the Mill as one of my under-managers so they could afford the cottage, but that's not going to happen now, so I want Nancy to have the job instead."

Lexie breathed out a sigh of relief.

"Well, good for her," she said, "I'm sure she'll do you proud."

There was a moment's awkward silence before Billy spoke again.

"Problem is, Lexie," Billy continued, "she's not used to office stuff, so I need someone to teach her 'show her the ropes' so to speak."

Lexie couldn't believe her ears.  "Show her the ropes!" she echoed, "you mean, come back to work at my old job again?"

"Would that be so bad?" Annie interrupted, seeing the look of horror on her daughter's face.

"Now the war's over," Billy chimed in, "you'll need to find work for yourself, so this would solve your problem as well."

Lexie leapt to her feet, panic now coursing through her body as their plan for her future crushed her heart.  "I don't HAVE a problem," she managed to blurt out, "I'm not staying in Dundee a moment longer than I have to and as for returning to Baxters.... .." she shook her head in disbelief, "the answer is NO."

Before any more could be said, Lexie ran from the room, leaving her mother and Billy Dawson floundering in her wake.

"What does she mean?" Annie asked, tearfully, "not staying in Dundee?" Billy knew Lexie.  He'd hoped he could kill two birds with one stone, find work for Nancy and keep Lexie home for Annie's sake, but Lexie's reaction had put paid to that.

"Hush now, Annie," he said gently, "she's tired, that's all," it'll be better in the morning, once she's had a chance to sleep on things."  But Billy knew it wouldn't be any better. He realised Lexie had plans of her own they knew nothing about and he'd have to think again about Nancy's future.

—-—oOo—-—

# Chapter 14

Billy Donnelly may have been back in Gladys Kelly's bed, but he knew he'd have work to do if he was to convince her to let him stay there.

He stared into the darkness as he relived his last meeting with Nancy, her cold words echoing in his heart.

THIS SHAM OF A MARRIAGE IS OVER.

He glanced at the figure of Gladys beside him, slumbering fitfully and snoring into her pillow. He'd made this bed and now he was going to have to lie in it, he realised grimly, his throat tightening at the thought at what he'd done and what he may have to do to survive.

He didn't sleep through the dark hours and when dawn broke, he crept out of the prostitute's bed and pulled on his crumpled clothes. He had to think a way out of the mess he had created and after swallowing a cup of cold water at the sink, he left the sleeping Gladys and inched down the creaking wooden staircase and into the bitter morning.

The Leerie's were already at work, dousing the gas street lamps as Billy made his way, head down, to the only place where he was still welcome, his mother's Lochee dwelling. He peered up at the tenement windows as he approached, sighing with relief that there was a faint glow of light at her window, his mother was awake.

He tapped softly on the door and whispered through the keyhole. "Mammy, it's me, Billy, open the door."

He could hear movement behind the door and after what seemed an eternity, the door knob turned and a shaft of light blinked through the crack.

"Billy?" he heard his mother's voice croak in disbelief. He hadn't seen her since she'd buried his father, but no matter, he was her son and blood was thicker than water after all, wasn't it?

"Let me in," he urged, pushing the door open further, "it's freezin' out here."

His mother stepped back, her hand flying to her throat, her pale eyes beginning to water as she saw her son standing before her.

"I thoucht you were dead" she murmured, her shaking hands reaching out to touch him, "you're no' a ghost are yea?"

Billy closed the door behind him, "no, mammy," he said, "it's really me," but he was shocked at the state of the shrunken woman in front of him, who was his mother. "I've been away fighting the war, but it's over now and I'm back home." He could feel the bones in her shoulders as he guided her back to her chair.

"How about I put the kettle on," he said, turning up the gas mantle and poking some life into the weak embers in the grate. But his mother had sunk back into her chair and he could see, she was in no state to help herself, let alone him.

Billy felt a twinge of shame at the sight of her. Since his father's death from Tuberculosis before the war, he'd barely thought about her or how she was managing on her own. He'd had enough to do, he told himself, in an attempt to assuage his guilt, what with Nancy and her 'carryings on' with Jim Murphy and three mouths to feed on his soldier's pay, he just didn't have the time, nor if truth be told, the inclination.

But now, the boot was on the other foot and her need was greater than his he decided, so now he would make up for his absence and maybe God would forgive him and he could hole up here till he could work out a way to get back to Nancy.

Gladys reached out to find the empty space left by Billy and blinked awake. She looked around the dimness of the single end before flopping back onto her pillow. "Gone already," she murmured to herself, wondering if she'd been too harsh on him, driving him away and not believing his protestations that he loved her. She got out of bed and opened the curtains at the tiny window. There was ice on the inside of the panes and she quickly shut them again.  Winter was truly here and she'd need the money she made running the brothel for Michael Flannaghan, to keep body and soul together.

She shivered into her shawl and set the fire with newspaper and sticks of wood to get it going before shovelling on some coal.  The fire began to take hold and she gazed at the flames as the heat touched her face.

Billy Donnelly didn't love her, she chided herself for being so foolish, not in a million years, she was on her own and her only hope of surviving was prostitution and Michael Flannaghan.

As she pushed herself upright, a flash of pain shot through her womb.  Gladys clutched her belly and inched back down into the chair.  The pain was happening more often and lasting longer each time, if she didn't know better, she'd have thought it was the start of labour pains.  She made a mental note to go to a doctor and ask about it, maybe get something for the pain, but as it eased again, she dismissed the idea and lit a cigarette. She'd have a cup of tea and some toast.  She'd be fine.

Nancy sat in the quiet of her home. Kevin was going to be fine and wee Billy and Mary Anne were bedded down for the night in the back room. The fire crackled in the grate as the clock ticked out the minutes of her life.  All of her bairns were safe and well, but Nancy had never felt so alone. She relived her last meeting with her husband, when her anger at his husband had boiled over and she'd sent him packing, but now, the anger had died down and had been replaced by emptiness and fear for the years ahead without him.

Her father would help, she knew, but now that Billy was gone, she didn't want to live at the Stannergate where she knew no one and besides, if she left Victoria Road, her husband would never be able to find her.

Nancy let the thought reverberate through her insides. After all that had happened, did she really want to see Billy again! She shook the thought and the feelings away, of course she didn't, her SHAM OF A MARRIAGE was well and truly OVER!

Lexie slammed the door of her bedroom firmly shut.  How

could Billy Dawson use her to make life easier for Nancy, she fumed? Didn't he realise, she had always been trouble and always would be? And as for her mother, well she just wanted Lexie to stay home forever and turn her into another Sarah Dawson!

Lexie paced the floor, muttering to herself about the unfairness of life, till her anger abated. There was no time to waste, so decided, as she unearthed her writing pad and pen from her suitcase and began her letter to Wing Commander Johnny Johnson at Lossiemouth.

*Dear Sir, she began, I hope you remember me and that you're still based at Lossiemouth. The reason I write is that I've been told that civilians are being recruited to replace enlisted personnel who have been demobbed and I was wondering if there were any positions available at the base that I would be suitable for.*

*I am at home in Dundee but would be more than happy to return to Lossiemouth to work and live.*

*Thank you in advance,*
*Yours truly*

Lexie re-read the letter and signed it. "Please God, let there be a way back to my life at Lossiemouth," she prayed, "and help my mother to understand I can't stay with her any longer."

Lexie sealed the letter and wrote the name and address on the front. She'd post it on the morning and in the meantime, try to get some sleep.

# Chapter 15

Annie's fingers were wrapped around her teacup, as she sipped the hot liquid and gazed into the middle-distance.  Did Lexie really mean it, she wondered anxiously, was she really going to leave Dundee and face the world alone?   There were more questions than answers, none of which she wanted to face. Billy's voice cut into her thoughts.

"Penny for them," he said, biting into his toast and marmalade.

Annie shrugged, dejectedly, "Why does she want to go so badly?" she asked Billy, turning worried eyes to meet his.

What was it with women, he wondered wearily, never happy with what they'd got and always thinking the grass was greener elsewhere.....

"She's young," he said, "and a free spirit, it would seem.  It's a pity Robbie Robertson was killed," he added, nodding his head in emphasis, "she'd have had a bairn or two to look after by now and all thoughts of wanting to leave Dundee would be out of her head."

Annie sighed.  She had been looking forward to being a grandmother and baking scones for her grand children, but the war had changed all that, her son Ian would be living in Carlisle, so any grandchildren would be too far away to visit and Lexie... ...well, she didn't seem to want anything other than find a way out of Dundee.

The sound of the kitchen door opening brought an end to any conversation as Lexie came into the room. She smiled weakly at her mother as she pulled out a chair and reached for the teapot.  Her letter to Johnny Johnson had been written and she was determined to post it that morning, no matter how much pressure she felt under to comply with the wishes of Billy Dawson to have her return to work at Baxters, albeit temporarily, in order to teach Nancy 'the ropes.'

Lexie felt her whole system tighten as the silence deepened till Billy finally broke into it. "Sleep well, Lexie?" he asked, amiably.

"Fine," she lied, sleep was becoming a thing of the past in Lexie's world but if she was ever going to feel 'normal' again, she knew she was going to have to break her mother's heart.

She poured herself a cup of tea and took a deep breath. "I've given your offer a lot of thought," she began, directing her attention at Billy, "but I've decided I'm going back to RAF Lossiemouth, as a civilian worker."

Her mother's eyes were bleak and fixed on Billy Dawson. Surely, he wouldn't let this happen, knowing how she felt about Lexie, surely, he'd persuade her to stay.

The seconds ticked by before Billy responded. "If that's your decision," he said formally, "then we wish you the best of luck and......." but before he could say any more, Annie pushed back her chair and ran from the room. All she wanted to do was to love her daughter, but it wasn't enough, Lexie hated her, she told herself, blamed her for destroying Josie McIntyre and marrying Billy Dawson, blamed her for the suicide of Lexie's father, Alex Melville, but most of all, blamed her for being a 'fallen woman' and bringing a bastard child into the world. All the pain of the past poured out of Annie in a wave of sobs, the only good thing she'd done in her life was to be Lexie's mother and now.....

Lexie made to run after Annie, but Billy stopped her, holding her shoulders tightly, "let it be," he said, "I'll look after her."

"But, she's upset," Lexie protested "and it's all my fault."

Billy could see the guilt in his step-daughter's eyes. He'd seen it before in his own eyes, when he'd told Josie that he was leaving her and going to be with Annie. He knew that, hard as the decision had been for Lexie to make, she had to go and he had to help her.

"Do what you have to do," he told Lexie "I'll make everything alright for your mother."

Before another word could be spoken, Lexie hurried to her room and packed the few belongs she had.  She sensed that further delay would be futile and she prayed that Billy Dawson would be true to his word and make everything alright for her mother.   She pushed the letter to Wing Commander Johnson into her handbag and with a last look at the closed door of her mother's bedroom, Lexie left the past behind and went out into the darkness of the early morning.  She would hand-deliver the letter to the Wing Commander, herself.

Billy made a fresh pot of tea and took a cupful through to Annie.

He sat down on the side of their bed and placed the cup on the bedside table.

"She's gone," he said, stroking her hair, "but I'm here Annie love," he whispered quietly, "you'll always have me."

Annie sniffed loudly and turned to face him.  Her eyes were red with weeping and her chin quivered with despair.

"Here," Billy said, handing her the cup of tea.  "She needs to run for a bit, Annie, that's all," he told her "but she'll be back when she's through running and you need to be strong now and ready to welcome her when that happens."

Annie took the cup and sipped the tea, leaning back against the headboard as the exhaustion of the emotional drain hit her, "do you really think she'll come back again?" she asked, her voice low and questioning.

"When the time's right for Lexie to return," Billy assured her, "nothing will keep her away."

The railway station was bleak and a cold wind blew along the platform as Lexie sat huddled on a bench, waiting for the first train to Inverness to arrive.  "It'll no' be here till nine o'clock," the station porter had told her, when she'd asked how long she'd have to wait.  A good two hours to go and the cold was already making its way from Lexie's feet to the rest of her legs.

She began to pace up and down the platform to keep warm and wished she'd eaten some breakfast before her hurried departure, but that hadn't been possible and if she was going to face life on her own, she reasoned, then this was going to be part of it. Going back to the warmth and safety of home wasn't an option.

The station clock ticked slowly onwards, every minute seeming like an hour, but eventually, the noise and steam from the arriving train blasted into the platform and Lexie, bleary-eyed and barely able to feel her feet, joined the other passengers boarding the transport to her future.

She found a space in the first carriage and sank into the corner of the seat, resting her head against the window and hoping the rest of the journey would be quiet enough for her to get some sleep. She closed her eyes as the slamming of carriage doors and the Station Master's whistle signalled their departure. Lexie was on her way.

Mary Anne and wee Billy had left for work and Kevin was happily toddling around Nancy's feet when her father knocked at her door.

She'd seen him pass by the window and immediately felt anxious. She knew he wanted her to leave Victoria Road and learn about 'office things' from Lexie, but she knew in her heart, she wanted none of it.

"You're about early," Nancy said, briskly, letting her father into the kitchen.

Billy took off his bonnet and picked up Kevin, who giggled with delight as he was raised into the air and perched on his grandpa's shoulders.

"Put him down," Nancy chided, smiling, "he's not long had his porridge and I don't want him being sick."

Billy lifted the child from his shoulders, and returned him to the floor, while his daughter turned her attention to making a fresh pot of tea.

No one spoke 'till the cups were filled and sugar and milk added, Billy not wanting to break the news about Lexie and Nancy not wanting to defy her father and his plan for her future.

"I've a bit of bad news," Billy said, finally, "about the job at Baxters."

Nancy held her breath, "bad news," she echoed, "how so?"

"Lexie's gone," he told her, "gone back to RAF Lossiemouth to work as a civilian or some such." He drank his tea before adding, "so, that means the job at Baxters can't happen and I'm afraid the cottage at Stannergate is off the table."

Nancy felt a wave of relief wash over her and she silently thanked Lexie for getting her 'off the hook.'

"That's a pity," she lied, "but I was thinking that maybe it would be better if I went back to the weaving instead and maybe Isabella Anderson could mind Kevin and with Mary Anne and wee Billy now working……

Billy blinked at the rush of information coming from his daughter.

"Well," he said, disbelief showing in his face, "that was quick, anyone would think you didn't really want to get a better life for yourself and the bairns."

Nancy felt herself colour. Of course she wanted a better life, but it had to be her way and for the first time in her life, she realised she didn't want to be answerable to anyone, not even her father.

She could see the look of hurt in his eyes and hastily began to gather up the tea things. "It's not that I don't appreciate all your help," she said, trying to sound reassuring, "because I do, it's just that……well…" Nancy turned to face her father, "I'm not your little girl anymore and……it's time I stopped expecting you to keep coming to my rescue…"

Mechanically, Billy nodded and pulled his bonnet on. "I hear you," he said, making to leave, "you know where to find me if you need me."

"Oh Dad!" Nancy cried, rushing to his side and throwing her arms around him. "It's not like that," she said worriedly, "I'll always need you, but I have to try to stand on my own two feet… …like Lexie," she finished lamely.

Billy couldn't avoid the truth of it. The war had changed everything, especially for the women of Dundee. Many had been forced to become the breadwinners, as their husbands hadn't come home from the fighting or had turned into

Spinsters as the shortage of eligible men had become more apparent.

"See you in the Weaving Flat when you're ready to start," Billy said, hugging her back. Nancy maybe wanted to be independent, but she still needed her father for some things and they both knew it.

Nancy blinked back a tear. "Thanks dad," she whispered, "for everything."

Billy turned down William Lane, crossed King Street and entered the offices of Baxters. The doorman saluted him, acknowledging his position as Mill Manager, "Good morning Sir," he said, "Your mail's on your desk."

Billy nodded without looking up at the doorman,"thanks Bert."

He climbed the stairs leading to his office and sat down behind his desk. Picking up the telephone he dialled the internal number for the Weaving flat. The clatter of the Weavers looms almost drowned out the voice of the Overseer. "Brannan."

"Mr Dawson here," Billy said, loudly, "a new Weaver will be starting in the next couple of weeks and I want you to make sure she gets a pair of looms and all the overtime she wants."

"Name," shouted John Brannan. "Donnelly," Billy said, "Nancy Donnelly."

"It'll be done Mr Dawson," the Overseer said, unquestioningly. When Mr Dawson wanted something done in the Weaving Flat, John Brannan made sure it happened. Billy ended the call and replaced the receiver in its cradle. The women in this post-war world maybe thought they didn't need men any more, but Billy and John Brannan knew otherwise.

———oOo———

# Chapter 16

It didn't take long for Billy Donnelly to realise that he couldn't depend on his mother for anything. She barely had enough food for herself, never mind him and was so weak, she'd be lucky to see the year out.

"I'll be back later," he told her, "bring some coal and bread and stuff."

His mother turned her aged eyes on him and Billy wondered if she even knew who he really was. He felt his heart sink, there was nothing else for it but to go back to Gladys.

He pulled the collar of his jacket up around his ears and cursed Billy Dawson, as the grimness of Lochee unfolded before him. If it hadn't been for his interfering, he was sure he could have talked Nancy round and be back in her warm bed by now. It was just a short walk to Gladys's single-end, but even that seemed to drain the little energy he had and he was eternally grateful to the woman, when she opened the door to him.

Gladys sniffed as he squeezed past her and into the room.

"Nae luck," she said, quickly closing the door to keep the warmth from the fire from escaping into the close.

"No luck?" he asked, quizzically, moving nearer to her, "what do you mean by that?"

Gladys shrugged. "Nae luck in gettin' back tae that wife o' yours?"

Billy flinched. Was he that obvious?

He feigned an injured look. He'd have to tread carefully, if Gladys threw him out, he'd be in serious trouble.

"You don't think…." he began "that I've been anywhere near the Viccy Road, do you?"

Gladys shrugged again. "Well, you werna' here when I woke up," she said, "so whut waz I supposed to think?"

"Gladys, Gladys," Billy murmured, "I was at my mother's house just two streets from here. She's no' well Gladys and I've been trying to find some way of buying her some food and coal to keep her going."

Gladys frowned. "You've never mentioned your mither afore," she said "and she lives jist roond the corner?"

Billy hung his head in mock shame. "I know," he said, "but what with the war and everything......you know.......things have been difficult for me."

"But no' as difficult as for your mither it would seem," Gladys retorted, feeling a ripple of compassion for the old woman's plight. Her own mother had wasted away before her eyes, despite Gladys's care and with her own daughter living somewhere in Aberdeen, she knew the fear of growing old and being alone.

Billy began to breathe easier. He realised he had hit a nerve and quickly pushed his advantage.

"So, if I'm not here," he said, "that's where I'll be."

Gladys nodded acceptance of the excuse. "Well, there's plenty coal in the bunker," she said, beginning to cut some bread for toasting, "maybee you could take'er a bucketfu' efter."

Billy felt a twinge of conscience, but not enough to stop him from asking Gladys if she could also spare a couple of shillings for some bread and tea for his mother as well.

The smell of burning toast brought any further discussion about Billy's mother to an end.

"You'd better hope trade at the brothel keeps up," Gladys told him, as she scraped the blackened breadcrumbs into the sink, "it looks like we're gonna need a bit mair money till you can find work."

WE, Billy thought in horror, there was no WE and WORK, the only work he was going to do was work at getting back with Nancy.

He fought back the urge to cut and run, but given his circumstances, he knew he had no choice but to stay. Gladys had to be kept sweet for now, but he'd have to work fast, before she began to believe he was there for the long haul.

She swept the slice of scraped toast onto the table in front of Billy, who'd suddenly lost his appetite.

"Brothel?" he queried, realising what Gladys had said, "since when?"

"Since Michael Flannaghan set me up to run things fur'im."

Billy felt his blood run very cold. "Michael Flannaghan," he repeated, his voice rising up a notch. "Not Mick Flannaghan, the Bookie from Polepark?"

Gladys nodded. "The same," she said, "do you ken 'im then?"

Billy knew him alright. Michael Flannaghan was responsible for nearly getting his father jailed for fraud years ago and if it hadn't been for the law throwing the case out on a technicality, he would have succeeded.

He pulled himself together, "we have a bit of history," Billy said, "so best not to mention my name to him."

Gladys brows furrowed in curiosity, "Owe him money, do you?" she asked.

"Something like that," Billy said, "so best to keep him in the dark about you and me."

You and me, Gladys thought, she liked the sound of that. Maybe things would go in her favour after all.

Toast eaten, he reminded Gladys about buying some food for his mother. She rummaged in the cloth bag she kept in the drawer of the sideboard and handed Billy half a crown.

"There," she said, "that should be enough to keep her fed for a couple o' days."

Billy pocketed the money and donned his coat. "Better get going," he said, kissing Gladys on the lips and hugging her closely, "I'll tell mum about your kindness."

Gladys felt herself relax in Billy's arms. No matter what he did, she still wanted his love and whatever he wanted so she could keep him with her, that's what she'd give him.

Billy hurried from the house and headed for the High Street. The tram into Dundee ground to a halt and he jumped on.

"Whar tae," the Conductor asked.

"Victoria Road," he said, settling down to watch the world go by as he planned his meeting with Nancy.

Nancy was singing to herself as she tidied the kitchen and got Kevin ready to go out. She knew that her Auntie Annie would be alone and probably missing Lexie, so now was a good time to visit and have a woman to woman chat about her going back to the weaving and maybe sound her out about Isabella Anderson minding Kevin.

She popped her son into his pram and bounced it down the stairs and out into Victoria Road. Nancy hadn't felt this good for a long time, but she should have known fate always seemed to have the knack of knocking her down just when she thought it was safe to put her head above the parapet. And the blow came in the form of her husband standing across the road from her, his hands dug deeply into his pockets and his face drawn and pale.

As he made to cross the road towards her, a tram blotted him from view and gave Nancy enough time to whisk Kevin from his pram and carry him back up the stairs. Her hand shaking, she turned the key in the lock and slammed the door shut behind her as Billy's boots sounded on the stairs running after her.

The door locked, Nancy hurried through to the back room, clutching Kevin in her arms. Her heart was hammering as she waited for the worst to happen. She knew he had the strength to break the door down and prayed that one of the neighbours would hear the noise and come to her rescue.

But the sound of splintering wood didn't happen, instead she heard Billy's voice pleading with her to open the door and let him in. He was so sorry and only wanted to make things better, he loved her and needed her, she just had to give him a chance to prove it.

Nancy set Kevin back on his feet and peeped around the room door.

She could see his shadow at the window through the net curtain. Part of her still wanted to believe him, but experience had taught her not to trust him and she quietly closed the door again and carried Kevin to the back room window. It overlooked

Victoria Road and she would wait there as long as it took, till she saw him cross the road again and get out of her life.

It was out of desperation that Nancy finally gave up the vigil and ventured back into the kitchen. The shadow had gone from the window and everything seemed quiet, but Nancy pulled the curtains tightly closed before daring to light the gas mantle and begin to put together some mash and butter for Kevin.

She lit the fire and felt her nerves ease as the warmth began to reach her bones. She felt sure Billy had gone and told herself to be more wary in future before venturing out, so it was with alarm that she heard a key turn in the lock and the door open.

Wee Billy's head peered into the gloom. "Why are the curtains shut?" he asked, pulling them open again. Nancy leapt up and closed them again, "to keep in the heat" she said hurriedly, "and what are you doing home so early?"

Wee Billy frowned, "we ran out o' Distemper, so the job's held up till the moarn and what was wee Kevin's pram doing at the foot o' the stairs?"

Nancy relaxed. "Sorry," she said, "I forgot about it….it's just that your dad was here earlier and…….."

A look of pure delight spread over wee Billy's face, before Nancy could say any more. "DAD!" he exclaimed. "Is he coming home at last?"

Nancy felt her eyes mist over. No matter how badly she felt she'd been treated by her husband, her son obviously thought the world of him. Telling him the truth about the future without his father in it wasn't going to be easy. And there was Mary Anne to consider, Nancy knew she was more grown up than wee Billy, but was she mature enough to want to never see her dad again?

"Get away with you now," Nancy said, dismissing her son's plea "and get those overalls off, the smell of paint is choking me."

She turned her back on her son and began peeling potatoes and onions at the sink, praying that Billy wouldn't return for if he did, wee Billy would surely let him in.

By the time Mary Anne got in from the Mill, the tea was ready and the family sat down to their sausages, mash and onion gravy, with Kevin being spoon fed by Nancy from her own plate.

They ate silently, as usual, but once the meal was over, Nancy decided to broach the subject of her going back to work at the Weaving, hoping that any talk of Billy's return would now be forgotten by her son.

"I was speaking to your Grandpa this morning," she began, trying to keep her voice positive "and he's suggested I go back to work at Baxters for a while, just till things get back to normal," she added, quickly "and now the war's over, lots of women are needed in the Mills and we could do with the extra money........" Nancy waited for their response, but both wee Billy and Mary Anne just smiled at her and there was no mention of their father as Mary Anne began to clear the table, and wee Billy put the kettle on to heat the water for the dish washing.

Nancy breathed a sigh of relief.  She would try again to go to Annie's tomorrow and hopefully enlist the help of Isabella Anderson to mind Kevin, but just when she thought she was 'out of the woods' she heard her son say to his sister, as they washed and dried the dishes...."so it looks like dad's coming back soon and maybe mum won't have to go back to work."

Nancy felt crushed.  So, now both of her children were expecting their father to return and any chance of a smooth road ahead was fading fast.

—·—oOo—·-—

# Chapter 17

The snow was falling thick and fast by the time the train pulled into Inverness Station.  There was no RAF truck to meet her this time and to walk in the snow to the camp was out of the question.  Lexie had met her first obstacle in her new independent life, how to keep from freezing to death on the station platform and finding a room for the night.

She hurried into the ticket office and knocked on the closed, wooden window.  The panel slid open and an annoyed face peered out at her.

"There's no' anither train oot o' Inverness till mornin'" he advised Lexie, preparing to close the window again.

"WAIT!" Lexie exclaimed, "I don't want a ticket," she blurted, "I need to know where I can get a room for the night and maybe some supper?"

The man's face softened, as he looked at the anxious face of the young woman.  "A bit stuck, are ye?"

Lexie nodded.  "I was hoping to walk to RAF Lossiemouth, but with the snow......"

"Give me a minute," the man said, closing the window again.

She could hear his muffled voice before the window opened and he re-appeared.

"The wife says that if you're stuck, you can bide wi' us for the nicht."

Lexie couldn't believe her ears.

"That would be just fine," she said, before he could change his mind

"and thank you for your kindness."

The man nodded, switched off the light and locked up the

station.  "Follow me," he said gruffly.

Lexie trudged after him, trying to walk in his footprints in the ankle-deep snow and, although the man's cottage wasn't far, her legs were aching by the time they got there.

The heat from the kitchen and the smell of something delicious cooking met them as the wife opened the door.

"Come away in," she said to Lexie, "my, but you look fair wabbitt."

Lexie felt a lump forming in her throat, the kindness of the couple to a complete stranger, threatening to bring her to tears.

"Supper's ready," she said, "Jock's favourite, Steak Pie."  She beamed at her husband, "and there's plenty to go roond, so you'll still get your fill."

The warmth of the welcome and the heat from the fire began to bring life back to Lexie and her icy feet.

"I can't thank you both enough," she said, as the steaming plate of food was placed in front of her.

"Goad lassie," Jenny Gilbert said, "if we canna help ane anither, then whaur would we be."

The conversation came to a halt, as Lexie ate every delicious mouthful of Jenny's steak pie and mashed tatties.

"That's better," Jock said, patting his stomach and turning his attention to Lexie.

"So, you're for the base the morn," he said, nodding thanks to Jenny as she placed a mug of tea in front of him.  "Are they expectin' you?"

Lexie shook her head.  "I was stationed there during the war and was hoping to find work again as a civilian."  She rummaged in her handbag and produced the letter addressed to Wing Commander Johnson.  "I'd meant to post this before making my way here, but circumstances......."

Lexie shrugged, by way of explanation, "so here I am."

Jock Gilbert blinked in surprise.  "Well, let's hope you've no' had a wasted journey."

Lexie grimaced, realising how difficult she had made it for herself by rushing out of Dundee, following her heart and not listening to her head.

Jenny Gilbert felt sorry for the girl, wondering what circumstances had forced her down this path and on her own too.

"A guid nicht's sleep is whut you need," she said to Lexie, nodding towards a door at the back of the kitchen, "thing's look better in the mornin'.

Lexie followed her into a tiny room with its box bed and one or two sticks of furniture. She lit the paraffin lamp and pushed a po' under the bed.

"Sleep well," her hostess said, "and remember things aye look better in the guid light o' day."

Lexie kicked off her shoes and flopped, fully clothed, onto the bed.

"Things will look better in the morning," she told herself, closing her eyes, or she was in trouble.

The next morning the snow had stopped and Lexie looked out of the tiny hole she had scrubbed clear in the frosted window, onto a white wonderland. Snow never looked like this in Dundee, it was always grey there with soot and grime that soon turned to icy slush.

She freshened up as best she could and straightened the bed covers. The Gilberts were already up and about and Jenny Gilbert was frying bacon and eggs in a huge iron frying pan when she came into the kitchen. Lexie marvelled at the sight, food shortages were still the order of the day in Dundee, but in the countryside it seemed that there was enough to eat for everyone.

"Sit yoursel' doon lassie," Jock said, "I've got a bit o' good news for ye."

Lexie pulled up a chair and waited expectantly.

"Wullie and his milkcart will be takin' milk up to the base in a wee while, and he's willin' to give ye a hurl to the camp."

Lexie couldn't believe her ears. Once again, overcome by the kindness of the Ticketmaster and his wife. "But that's wonderful Mr Gilbert," she grinned, "I must admit I wasn't looking forward to the walk."

"Well, hurry up and eat your breakfast," Jenny said, placing yet another plate of delicious food in front of her, "Wullie doesna' like to be kept waitin'.'

Lexie didn't need to be told twice and soon the bacon and eggs, as well as toast and jam were eaten and Lexie was gathering her meagre belongings together, ready to join Wullie on his milk cart taking her on the next stage of her journey towards her new life.

'I can't thank you enough,' Lexie said, reaching into her handbag for her purse. Whatever it cost, it would be worth it, Lexie reasoned, but Jock and Jenny Gilbert would have none of it.

'Put that away,' Jock Gilbert said, firmly, pushing Lexie's purse back into her handbag. 'There's nae charge for onything,' he said, a mist of tears forming in his eyes as he looked at the young girl in front of him. How the world had changed since the war, the old values he and his wife had lived by, seemed to be diminishing daily and the future for girls, like Lexie, he couldn't begin to comprehend.

The whinnying of Wullie's horse brought him back to the moment.

'Here's yir hurl,' he said, gruffly, carrying Lexie's small bag to the door, followed by Lexie and Mrs Gilbert.

Jock helped her up onto the cart and they waved her off with a cheery smile. 'I hope she finds whut she's lookin' for,' Jock said, shaking his head and guiding Jenny back into the warmth of the kitchen.

His wife patted his arm. 'She's got this far,' she said, fleetingly wishing that she had had the courage to be independent when she was young, but knowing that her Jock was a good man, without whom she wouldn't have the happy life she enjoyed. 'She'll be fine.'

Lexie felt increasingly anxious as Wullie and his milk cart trundled through the snow towards the Base and her head began to fill with doubts and fears. What if Wing Commander Johnson didn't even remember her, what if they didn't hire civilian workers, what if she had to go back to Dundee, beaten at the first hurdle!

'We're here,' Wullie announced as the camp gate came into view, putting an end to Lexie's train of thoughts.

With just a cursory glance at her identification card, the guard flagged Lexie and Wullie through and she breathed a sigh of relief as she jumped down from the cart. It was all so familiar and felt like she was coming home.

"Thanks," she called to the milkman, but he was already unloading the churns and rolling them to the cookhouse door.

Lexie headed for the Administration Block and the Wing Commander's office. It was now or never, she told herself, as the nerves returned with a vengeance.

"Can I speak with Wing Commander Johnson?" Lexie asked the young girl behind a desk, noting she wasn't in uniform.

"Name?" she asked briefly, picking up the desk telephone.

"Sergeant Melville," Lexie said, "well, ex-sergeant," she added.

The girl repeated her name into the receiver and Lexie held her breath.

"You've to go in immediately," the girl said, pointing to a door and replacing the receiver before returning to her typing.

Lexie knocked on the door and heard Johnny Johnson's voice call "Enter" from the other side.

Lexie pushed open the door. If she had any doubts that Wing Commander Johnson had forgotten her, they were quickly dispersed as he came around the side of his desk and shook her hand warmly.

"Sergeant Melville," he beamed, "what a lovely surprise."

Lexie felt a rush of colour to her face. All protocol seemed to have gone out of the window, as Johnny Johnson ushered her to a chair and telephoned for tea and biscuits to be brought in.

"You're looking well," he said, before remembering that she had lost her husband at sea, "I mean," he added sympathetically, "considering what you've had to deal with."

Lexie nodded appreciatively, before producing the letter she had written to him but never posted. "I thought I'd better hand deliver this," she said, "in case you'd forgotten who I was."

The Wing Commander took the envelope, surprised that she would think she'd been forgotten so easily. He opened It while Lexie waited.

Johnny Johnson placed the letter in front of him, his face

unsmiling and concerned.

"I wish you'd posted this to me," he said, as Lexie's heart began to sink, "and saved yourself the journey."

Lexie could feel huge tears welling in her eyes. How foolish and stupid she had been to think that all she had to do with make her way back to Lossiemouth and all her troubles would be over.

There was a knock at the door and the girl from the desk came in, pushing a small trolley with the tea and biscuits on it. She looked quizzically at the Wing Commander and his tearful visitor.

"Just leave it there," Johnny Johnson said, "we'll help ourselves."

"I'm so sorry," he said, turning his attention back to Lexie, "we do use civilians for some work, but it's only a few and the vacancies are filled, very quickly, by local workers."

Lexie tried to gather herself together, berating herself for putting all her eggs in one basket and rushing headlong into things without any contingency plan. Had she learned nothing in the WAAF, except how to fall in love with the wrong man!

She made to stand up, but her legs wobbled beneath her and she bumped back down into the chair.

"A cup of tea wouldn't go amiss, I think," Johnny Johnson said, anxiously, going over to the trolley and beginning to pour out the tea.

"I'm so sorry I couldn't be of help to you," he said, handing her the tea and racking his brains for something to say to comfort her.

"You're quite welcome to stay on the base overnight" he said, hoping the snow wouldn't get any worse, " you could bed down in the Hospital Wing and I'll arrange for a truck to take you back to Inverness Station tomorrow."

Lexie felt crushed. "Thanks," she whispered, her fingers gripping the teacup like a life raft "and I'm sorry to have been a bother to you."

The Wing Commander lifted the telephone again, and summoned the girl again.

"Sylvia," he said on her return, "why don't you take some time off and show Miss Melville around a bit, especially the Hospital Wing and maybe have some lunch in the Canteen."

If Sylvia was surprised, she didn't show it and smiled encouragingly at Lexie to follow her. Lexie felt like a fish out of water, what had made her believe that she could just change out of her uniform and into civilian wear and everything would go back to the way it was before.

She thanked Johnny Johnson, dejection sitting like a black crow on her shoulders and followed the girl out of his office. She waited while Sylvia pulled on her coat and hat, not really caring about anything anymore, except having to go back to Dundee with her tail between her legs, her big plan for the future in ruins.

"Thanks for volunteering to show me around," Lexie said, sounding dejected, "but I already know the Base."

Sylvia could see Lexie's heart wasn't in it. "How about we go for a hot drink in the Canteen then and get out of this cold. Lexie nodded and followed the girl into the old NAAFI. There were new tables and chairs and the paintwork had been freshened, but for Lexie it was just as it used to be and memories of Bo McGhee suddenly came rushing back.

She hadn't thought about the Canadian for a long time now and was surprised at how vivid her recollection of him was.

She had been sailing to Halifax in Canada to marry him, when the past, in the shape of Robbie Robertson had changed all that and she'd married Robbie aboard his ship instead. Lexie felt tears of loss begin to form when Sylvia's voice interrupted them.

"Penny for them," she said, spooning sugar into her cup.

Lexie blinked. "Sorry," she said, "just memories."

"Do you want to talk about it" Slyvia asked, kindly.

Before she could stop herself, Lexie poured out the whole story about Bo, Robbie and life in Dundee.

"So," she concluded, "I can't go back there and I need to find work quickly or that's what will happen."

Sylvia frowned. "You know what they say," she said gently,

"the darkest hour is just before the dawn and something will turn up, if it's meant to be."

Lexie took a deep breath and hoped Sylvia was right, but in the meantime, she decided she would spend the night at the Base, all of the travelling and talking had drained her emotionally and some quiet time and rest was what she needed most.

Sylvia walked with her to the Hospital Wing and explained the situation to the duty nurse. "I'll tell Wing Commander Johnson that you'll be staying the night," she told Lexie "and I'm sure things will be better in the morning," she added, as she left to go back to her duties.

Lexie almost laughed. She'd heard that just the day before from Jenny Gilbert, but things hadn't been better in the morning, in fact, they'd been worse.

She wrapped herself in a blanket and curled up on the hospital bed. It was 3 o'clock when Lexie woke up and the winter sky was already darkening. She could hear the sounds of the nurses going about their duties and realised this was the same room she'd been in when she'd been brought back to the Base after being involved in the rescue of the crew of the ditched Wellington Bomber. They'd given her an Empire Medal for her bravery and she'd had to go to Edinburgh for the Presentation. And that's when fate had brought Bo McGhee and Lexie together.

Images of Rainbow McGhee flooded her mind and she smiled as she remembered their first meeting at RAF Lossiemouth. "The name's McGhee," he'd said, "Captain Rainbow McGhee, but my friends call me Bo."

Lexie didn't want to remember any more, Bo was in the past and that's where he would stay. She shook off the blanket and freshened up at the little sink in the corner of the room. She'd go back to the Canteen, have some food and then sleep till morning. Tomorrow would arrive and she'd have to deal with whatever it brought and sometimes, she reasoned, you have to take a step back before you can go forward again.

She was just about to leave the room when a nurse knocked and came in.

"Miss Melville," she said, "Wing Commander Johnson would like you to join him for dinner at his Quarters at 1800 hours."

Lexie sat back down on her bed in surprise. The Wing Commander had been kind enough to her and she didn't want to outstay her welcome, but before she could refuse, the nurse added, "and he says it's an order!"

Had he forgotten Lexie was a civilian now, she mused. "In that case," she said, smiling, "let him know I'll be there."

The moon was reflecting off the snow giving enough light to guide Lexie to Johnny Johnson's Quarters and dinner. She hadn't eaten since breakfast at Jock Gilbert's and was starving and just a bit nervous at dining with the Wing Commander.

"Enter," he called out as she knocked at his door. Lexie eased the door open and felt the warmth of the room waft over her cheeks.

"Come in," Johnny Johnson smiled, "dinner will be served directly," he said in mock seriousness.

Lexie couldn't help but grin and took her seat opposite him at his table.

He lifted a decanter of red wine and proceeded to pour out two glasses, handing one to Lexie.

"Here's to bad news and good news," he said, raising his glass and urging Lexie to do the same.

Confused, Lexie sipped at the wine, repeating the strange toast.

The door opened and a young man in RAF uniform wheeled in a trolley of food. "Leave it there," the Wingco said, "and thank you, but we'll serve ourselves."

The dinner was delicious and Lexie relaxed as Johnny Johnson regaled her with tales of his wartime sorties and it wasn't till they'd left the table and were seated in two armchairs that the Wing Commander spoke of the real reason for the invitation to dinner.

"I know I gave you some bad news earlier today" Johnny Johnson began, pouring himself a measure of whiskey "and I'm sorry about that, but I made one or two telephone calls this afternoon and, if you are open to an alternative to working at RAF Lossiemouth, I think I may have something of interest to you."

Lexie was intrigued and sat forward in her chair.

"A very dear friend of mine, Wing Commander Martin Kettlewell, has just taken over command at RAF Montrose and......" Lexie's eyes widened.

"he needs a Private Secretary to get his office up and running and...."

Lexie held her breath. "I said you might very well fit the bill."

Lexie was speechless. "So," Johnny Johnson said, a twinkle in his eye, "do I take it you're interested?"

Lexie nodded vigorously. "Interested?" she managed to echo, "I could think of nothing I'd rather be doing......except, of course, working here."

"That's settled then," the Wing Commander said, "I'll tell him you'll report to RAF Montrose on Friday and you can both decide if it's the job for you."

Lexie felt she was floating on a cloud as she made her way back through the snow to the Hospital Wing. Friday was only three days away and she had to get back to Dundee and prepare for the interview of her life.

She wouldn't be far from her mother and Billy, she reasoned, but far enough to feel her life was her own again.

"Isn't it wonderfrul," she whispered to the moon, hugging herself with joy. And Jenny Gilbert was right after all, things do look different in the morning and tomorrow morning would be very different indeed from the one she'd just lived through.

Lexie couldn't wait.

———oOo———

# Chapter 18

Nancy craned her neck taking in the sweep of Victoria Road. There was no sign of her errant husband and she quickly pulled on her coat and hat and wrapped a thick scarf round Kevin's neck, crossing it over his chest and pinning it at his back.

"There," she said, smiling at her toddler, "that'll keep Jack Frost away and let's hope it keeps your daddy away too," she added, grimly, "today she had to make sure Isabella Anderson could mind her son, for tomorrow, she was heading for the Weaving Flat at Baxters to find work.

But the coast was clear and Nancy hurried along Victoria Road and up Dura Street, heading for Annie's house in Albert Street.

Although the weather was icy, by the time Nancy reached Annie's door, she was hot with the exertion of pushing Kevin in his pram through the frozen slush on the pavements.

"Come away in," Annie beamed, if her own daughter didn't appreciate her, then her niece certainly did. "I've just made a batch of pancakes and there's still the last of the jam in the pantry," she said, unpinning Kevin's scarf and removing his coat.

"But what's brought you out in this weather?" Annie asked, "not that I'm not pleased to see you both," she added, quickly.

Nancy draped her coat over one of the kitchen chairs and pushed her dark hair back into place.

"You know I always love visiting you," Nancy smiled "and me and Kevin wouldn't say no to a pancake and jam, but there's something a bit more urgent I need to speak to you about."

Annie's brows furrowed, "the bairns are all fine aren't they?"

"Yes, yes," Nancy assured her, "but dad visited this morning and he tells me that Lexie's left home and......" The creases in Annie's brow deepened and her mouth tightened at the memory of Lexie's going.

"She's a grown woman now," Annie said, tightly, "or so she thinks and she's gone off to Lossiemouth to work at the RAF Base there."

Nancy waited till Annie composed herself again and began spreading the pancakes, giving the first one to Kevin who tried to eat the treat whole, resulting in raspberry jam all over his mouth.

Annie tossed Nancy a damp cloth. "Did he have his breakfast?" she asked, as the bairn reached out for another pancake.

Nancy felt her face colour and knew how Lexie must have felt, being treated like a child by Annie all those years, but she needed her support now if she was to get back to work.

"Sorry," she said instead, "I think it's the cold making him hungrier than usual."

Annie seemed to accept the answer and poured out their tea, as Nancy steered the conversation back to the real reason for her visit.

"It looks like I have to say goodbye to the cottage in the Stannergate," Nancy said, chattily, "and the job as an Under Manager at Baxters."

Annie's eyes filled with concern. Was nothing ever going to go right for her niece?

"But how are you going to manage without Billy," she said, "is it really all over between the two of you?"

It was Nancy's turn to frown. "I'm afraid it is Auntie Annie," she whispered, "so I've no option but to get back to work myself, at the weaving."

Annie sat back in surprise. "But what about Kevin.....?"

Nancy took her chance. "That's what I wanted to ask you about," she said hurriedly, "I was wondering if Isabella could mind him for me?"

There, it was out and silence filled the room, except for the sudden sound of knocking at the door.

Annie got up to answer it, "you can ask her yourself," she said, "she always drops by on Wednesday for tea and pancakes."

Isabella Anderson bustled into the room, her Salvation Army Bonnet wedged on her head and her black uniform covered by a long, matching overcoat.

Her eyes lit up when she saw Kevin and Nancy and was pleased that Annie still had her niece and her family around her. Billy had telephoned her and told her of Lexie's decision to return to Lossiemouth and she knew Annie would be hurting.

"And is this wee one all better now?" she asked Nancy, "we were all a bit worried about you," she crooned to Kevin, tickling him under the chin.

Annie spread more pancakes with the jam and brought another cup to the table for Isabella.

"How are things at the Hall Mrs Anderson?" Nancy asked, cordially, "I can see the place from my back window and there always seems to be a stream of people going out and in."

Isabella took off her bonnet and pulled up the last chair at the table.

"That'll be the mums," she told Nancy, "they bring their wee ones along and we mind them while they're at work."

Nancy couldn't believe her ears. "You mean, you look after ALL of them, like in a nursery?" Isabella grinned. "Don't look so shocked," she said, "since the war, so many women have had to go back to work in the Mills and well, there was a need and the Salvation Army met it."

Both women looked at Annie, Isabella waiting for her confirmation and Nancy waiting for her to breach the subject of minding Kevin, but Annie did neither, her thoughts returning again to the absence of her own daughter.

Isabella noticed it first. "Are you alright Annie?" she asked, "maybe planning your Christmas baking?"

But Annie shook her head. "Christmas!" she said, sadly, "there'll be no Christmas in this house, not with Lexie gone."

Even King Kevin seemed to sense the change in the air and stopped banging a teaspoon on the table.

Isabella sighed. "I thought you might be feeling low," she said, "but we've talked about this before and you know Lexie has to do what she thinks is best for her," she counselled, kindly, reaching out for Annie's hand.

Nancy lifted Kevin up and made to leave, she could see that Annie needed to talk with Isabella and now wasn't the time to pursue her own agenda.  Later, she would go over to the Salvation Army Hall in Wellington Street and see Isabella there about taking Kevin into the fold."

"Thanks for the tea and pancakes," she said quietly, making her way out of the kitchen, almost to the oblivion of Annie. Isabella nodded her understanding and returned her attention to her sister-in-law.

"Now, now, Annie," she said, "there's no good hanging on to the past,
one way or another, Lexie's decided to make her own way in the world and that's her right."  Annie said nothing.

"She's been through a war Annie," Isabella tried again to get Annie to understand her daughter's need for freedom and had Robbie not been killed, she'd be a married woman, probably with young 'uns of her own and away from home anyway."

Eventually, Annie nodded, "I know," she said, "it's just……it's just I miss her and she was the only good thing that came from my marriage to Alex..."Annie began to falter.  Alex Melville was Isabella's brother and she'd witnessed his cruel treatment of Annie during their marriage.

Isabella's heart went out to her and she reached out and took her hand.

"Sssshhh, now," she said, I know what you're saying, but don't make that the reason for clinging to Lexie."

Annie sighed, "I'll try," she said, getting up from the table and starting to clear away the tea things, "I'll make us a fresh pot of tea."

Isabella relaxed.  "And how's Nancy and her brood?" she asked, changing the subject away from Lexie.

"She says she's going back to work," Annie told her, "to the weaving again."

"Well, that's wonderful!" Isabella exclaimed.  She'd seen for herself Billy Donnelly's behaviour when Kevin was in hospital and could well understand that Nancy had seen him off. Unfortunately, without a husband, she had left herself in a vulnerable position, so getting herself back to work, Isabella knew, would be the best thing she could do.

"She can only go to work if someone can mind Kevin though," Annie told her, pouring out a cup of freshly brewed tea and handing it over to Isabella.

Without giving it a second thought, Isabella immediately volunteered.

"She can leave him with me," she said, "join in the fun at the Hall with the other bairns."

Annie smiled. Nothing was ever too much trouble for her sister-in-law.

"There's room for another one?" she asked.

"There's plenty of room," Isabella said, enthusiastically, "and while we're on the subject, we could also do with another volunteer helper?"

Annie's eyes widened. "You mean, ME?"

"And why not," Isabella said, "better than sitting around here fretting."

Annie knew she was right. "I'll speak to Billy about it when he comes home but, yes, I think I'd quite like that."

The two women toasted the decision with cups of tea and for the first time since Lexie left, Annie felt a moment of happiness for the future.

Nancy didn't want to go back to Victoria Road and instead made her way down Princes Street and into Baxters Office.

"Is Mr Dawson in?" she asked the doorman. "He is."

Nancy nodded, "can you let him know I'm here and need to speak to him?"

The doorman signalled to the girl in the Reception Office to telephone Mr Dawson. Two minutes later, Nancy was sitting in her father's office while his Secretary looked after Kevin.

"So, you've not changed your mind," Billy said, "and I suppose you want me to arrange to get you back at the Looms." Nancy blinked. "Please."

This wasn't how Billy had planned his daughter's future, but it would be better than having to take back that liar of a husband of hers.

"And what about Kevin" Billy said, "who's to be minding him?"

"Isabella," Nancy quickly lied, "I spoke to her just a wee while ago and she's fine about it."

Billy frowned. "Are you sure?"

"Very sure," Nancy replied, her fingers crossed tightly in her lap.

Reluctantly, Billy picked up the telephone and dialled the number of the Weaving Flat.

"Mr Dawson here," he began, when John Brannan answered, "that Weaver we talked about will be starting with us next……
.Monday?" he queried Nancy.  Nancy smiled widely and nodded vigorously.

"I'll send her down now, so you can meet her," Billy continued, "so make sure you look after her."

John Brannan flicked through his notebook, Mr Dawson was going to an awful lot of trouble for this Weaver, he mused, finding the name he'd scribbled down a few days previously. "Nancy Donnelly," he muttered "yes, that was the name, Nancy Donnelly."

Her father's secretary happily agreed to look after Kevin while Nancy went down to the Weaving Flat.  As she pushed through the rubber doors, the racket of the looms assailed her ears and the smell of jute flooded her nostrils.  Women, old and young, were bent to their task and the Weaving Flat was a hive of industry.  Nancy could see the back of the Overseer working at his desk and made her way through the noise to meet him.

"MR BRANNAN," she shouted attracting his attention. "Nancy Donnelly," she announced herself.

John Brannan indicated the door out of the Flat, pointing to his ears.  Nancy nodded and followed him.  He wanted to know more about Nancy Donnelly and why she was so important to Mr Dawson.

He took in her dark eyes and hair, her trim figure and the smooth skin on her pale face, unlike the other Weavers, their faces lined and blotched.

"Don't I know you?" he asked, "your name sounds kind'a familiar."

"Don't think so," Nancy replied. She'd have remembered meeting John Brannan, with his military stature and confident eyes.

"I worked here long ago," she said, "but with the war and everything, I need to get back to earning again."

John nodded his understanding. "I did my stint with the Scots Guards," he said, "but I'm glad it's over and things can get back to some kind of normality."

Nancy flinched. John Brannan had been in the Scots Guards, like her husband! Hoping they'd never met, she quickly changed the subject.

"So, is there a pair of looms needing a Weaver?" she asked.

"There is," John said, "and what's more, Mr Dawson insists you get them, along with all the overtime you want."

Nancy could see, he was confused about all the attention she was getting and decided to come clean.

"Mr Dawson's my father, if you must know," she said, tilting her chin up and straightening her back "and I'd appreciate if you'd just treat me like all the other Weavers. I don't want any favours."

John Brannan smiled, Nancy Donnelly had guts, he'd give her that and whether her father wanted her to get special treatment or not, he was going to make sure she got it.

He glanced down at her left hand. No wedding ring, he noticed and wondered why a lovely woman like Nancy Donnelly was single. Perhaps she had been married and her husband hadn't come back from the war, he pondered, which was lucky for him.

"Is everything alright," Nancy asked, bringing John back from his wonderings.

"Fine," he said quickly, "everything's fine." He guided her back into the Weaving Flat and quickly included her name in his Register and worksheets.

"See you next Monday," he mouthed. Nancy nodded. This

was it, she beamed, she was going to be a Weaver again and couldn't wait.

She hurried back to her father's office and picked up Kevin, who was scribbling on a sheet of typing paper with the Secretary's pencil and reluctant to leave.

"C'mon," Nancy chided him, "time to go."  She handed the pencil back and carried him downstairs to Baxters Entrance and his pram.

Tomorrow, she would go and see Isabella at the Salvation Army Hall about minding Kevin and by next Monday, she'd be a Weaver again.

Nancy sang to herself as she pushed Kevin back up William Lane and on to Victoria Road, her mind picturing her return to work and savouring the freedom and money that that would bring.

She was just about to turn into the close when wee Billy came running up behind her.

She'd never seen him so happy as he put an arm around her. "Guess who I just met?" he said, "at the Wellgate steps."

Nancy lifted Kevin out of his pram, while her son took control of manoeuvring the pram up the stairs to their home.

"Well, whoever it is," Nancy grinned, "you should see her more often."

Wee Billy laughed.  "It's not a girl," he said, "it was DAD."

Nancy felt her blood run cold.  Why was it, just when everything seemed to be going right for her, it started to go wrong.  She forced down the surge of panic, "and what did he have to say for himself?"

"Not a lot," wee Billy called over his shoulder as he made his way through to the back room, "but I'm meeting him in the Thrums at six o'clock and he's......."

"YOU CAN'T MEET HIM," Nancy said loudly, "not at six o'clock and not ever."

Wee Billy came back into the kitchen, his eyes levelling with his mother's.

"He's my dad," he said, almost coldly "and I want to see him, so I'll be going."

Nancy sat down at the kitchen table, "we need to talk," she said "I need you to listen to what I have to say and to understand why you can't see you dad."

Reluctantly, wee Billy sat down and Nancy told him everything, including his father's carryings on with Gladys Kelly and his broken promises to stay away from her.  Wee Billy sat in silence till Nancy had finished.  He had no questions for her, nor showed any emotions, as he pushed his chair back and stood up.

"Thanks for telling me," he said, "but now I'm going to meet dad and hear his side of the story."

Nancy watched as her son washed his face and hands at the sink and pulled on his jacket.

"Remember I love you," she called to his back as he closed the door quietly behind him.  But wee Billy didn't want to hear these words from his mother, he wanted to hear them from his father.

# Chapter 19

The train journey from Lossiemouth was arduous and cold. Lexie sat huddled in the corner of the empty carriage, her legs tucked under her and her coat collar pulled up around her neck. But, she couldn't have been happier, she was so glad that she'd decided to go to Lossiemouth herself instead of posting the letter to the Wing Commander, or the chance of working at RAF Montrose probably wouldn't have happened.

She'd speak to Winnie as soon as she could, but before that, she was going to have to tell her mother her news and, she knew, she wouldn't be happy about it.

The weather in Dundee hadn't been as bad as Lossiemouth, with its snow drifts and icy wind, but Lexie was exhausted by the time she'd walked from the bus station, through the frozen, grey slush, to her home in Albert Street.

"Lexie!" Annie called out in shock at the sight of her red-nosed daughter and hurried her into the lobby. "Why, you're frozen stiff," she said, anxiously "and where have you been?"

Lexie tried to hush her with a wave of her hand as she unwound her scarf and struggled out of her winter coat. "Can I get warmed up first, please," she begged her mother, wishing she could just crawl into bed with a hot water bottle.

"She's home, she's home," Annie kept murmuring and that was all that mattered. Billy had been right, 'she'll come home when she's ready', he'd said and here she was.

Two cups of hot tea and four of her mother's pancakes later, Lexie began to warm up.

"When does Billy get home from the Mill?" she asked, not wanting to confront her mother alone and hoping that he would understand and support her when she broke the news of her leaving, yet again.

She felt that it always seemed to be she was leaving Dundee, but like it or not, she kept being driven back there.  But this next time, would be different, there would be no coming back.

"About now," Annie said, "it depends on how well the Overseers have tallied the yardage. Why do you ask" Annie queried, worriedly, "you're not rushing off already are you?"

The question hung in the air.  There was no time like the present and Lexie 'grasped the nettle.'

"No yet," she said, trying to sound nonchalant "I'll know when I'm going by tomorrow."

Annie felt her heart sink lower and lower as her daughter told her about Lossiemouth, Wing Commander Johnson and the job at Montrose.

"And, it's only a few miles away," she warbled on, not giving Annie a chance to try to stop her, "so I'll manage to come home now and then..."

Lexie stopped speaking.  This wasn't what her mother wanted to hear and she could feel herself begin to wilt.  Why was she so anxious to leave Dundee anyway, she asked herself, what was wrong with things just as they were......but Lexie knew, deep down, she had to leave this place if she was ever going to find love and happiness in her life.

The return of Billy from the Mill eased the tension and Lexie rushed to help him off with his coat and bonnet.

"Well, here's a surprise," he smiled, looking at Annie and trying to gauge the situation.

"She's not staying long," Annie said, tightly, "she's off to Montrose in the morning, chasing some silly dream of happiness....." Annie took off her apron.  "I'm going for a walk," she said, "alone."

Before Billy or Lexie could stop her, she was gone.

"Will she be alright?" Lexie asked bleakly.  "She can't seem to see that I'm not her little girl anymore and that......"

"Hush now, Lexie," Billy said, "she knows you're all grown up now, but she's just taking a little while getting used to the idea."

Billy pulled up a chair beside her. "Tell me about Montrose," he said "and don't worry about your mother, leave that to me."

Annie hurried out of the house, tears threatening to fall and made her way to Isabella's. If there was one person who would understand how she felt it was her.

A surprised Isabella ushered her in. "I didn't expect to see you again so soon," she said, "there's nothing wrong I hope?"

Annie shook her head, eyes downcast, she just wanted her daughter back, was that too much to ask?

Isabella sat her down and took her hand. "What's Lexie been up to now?" she asked, gently, not really needing to ask. Poor Lexie, she thought, struggling to make a new life for herself and Annie, struggling to let her go.

Annie took a deep breath and gripped Isabella's hand tighter.

"She's going to work at the RAF Base at Montrose," she said, "but she may as well be on the other side of the world for all I'll see of her."

It was Isabella's turn to tighten her grip on Annie's hand. It was worrying that Annie seemed so unable to let Lexie go.

"Now, that's not so bad is it?" Isabella asked, "I'm sure she'll manage to visit when she can and, anyway, you'll be too busy helping with the bairns at the Hall, you won't have time to miss her."

Annie shrugged and seemed to fold in on herself. "You can't take on like this, Annie," Isabella said, concern growing for her sister-in-law, "you'll make yourself ill."

Annie shrugged again but said nothing.

Isabella patted her hand. "I'll just get us some tea," she said, "I'll be back in a couple of jiffs."

Isabella hurried from the room, picked up the telephone and dialled Billy Dawson's number.

"I'll get it," Lexie called, glad of the distraction.

"Lexie," Isabella said, recognising her voice, "is Billy with you?"

"Yes," Lexie said, "I'll just get him."

Lexie covered the mouthpiece with her hand. "It's Isabella," she said "and she sounds worried."

Billy put the telephone to his ear and listened, his face darkening.

"I'll be right over," he said, quickly replacing the receiver and reaching for his coat from the hallstand.

"What's wrong?" asked Lexie, anxiously, "is Isabella alright?"

Billy placed his hands on her shoulders. "Isabella's fine," he said, "I'm just going to collect Annie" and before Lexie could ask anything more, Billy was gone.

Annie was lying on the sofa in the living room, a woollen blanket draped over her when Billy arrived.

"There's something wrong Billy," Isabella said quietly "and it's more than just wanting Lexie to stay." Billy felt a stab of fear. "I think she needs to see a doctor," Isabella counselled, "and soon."

Billy pulled up a chair beside Annie and stroked her hair. "What's wrong with my girl then?" he asked trying not to read too much into the paleness of her skin and the empty look in her eyes.

Tears began to well in Annie's eyes, "I don't know, Billy," she whispered, "......I'm scared'!"

Billy leant closer to hear her better. "There's no need to be scared," he said, softly, "you know I wouldn't let anything hurt you."

But Annie wasn't listening, she just wanted to sleep and for all the hurt to go away. Billy watched as she closed her eyes, her knuckles tightly gripping the blanket. Isabella was right, something was very wrong.

He found Isabella in the kitchen. "Can Annie stay tonight?" he asked, "I don't want Lexie to see her like this and tomorrow, I'll get Dr McFarlane to come in and have a look at her."

Isabella agreed. "I'll look after her," she assured him, "and please tell Lexie she must go to Montrose tomorrow, for if she doesn't, she'll have lost everything she's fought for and deserves."

Billy sat in his motor, not wanting to have to go home and lie to Lexie, but not wanting to tell her the truth either. Annie was ill and the cure was for Lexie to stay, but he couldn't sacrifice her happiness for the woman he loved, just as he couldn't sacrifice his own happiness by staying with Josie.

He started up the engine.  One thing was sure, there would be no winners and maybe this was God's way of punishing him for deserting Josie and the girls to be with Annie.

He pushed the toxic thought from his head.  Somehow, Lexie had to go to Montrose in the morning and he had to get Annie well again.

Lexie was waiting anxiously for Billy's return with her mother, but when Billy returned alone, her anxiety heightened.

"What's going on?" she asked, "where's mum?"

Billy had to think quickly.   "She's with Isabella," he said truthfully, "but she's had a fall......a trip more like," he lied, "so she's staying the night and the Doctor will have a look at her in the morning."

Lexie felt her shoulders relax.  "But, she's alright?"

"She's fine," Billy assured her, "just had a bit of a fright, that's all.  Doctor McFarlane will sort things tomorrow, but you need to be up early tomorrow yourself for your trip to Montrose, so best get some sleep eh?"

Billy had said all of this with his back to Lexie, as he dried some crockery at the sink, fearful of looking at her, lest she law the lie written in his eyes, but when he turned to say goodnight to her, she'd already gone.

Wearily, Billy made a pot of tea and lit a cigarette.  All the hopes he had for a 'happy ever after' world, seemed to have vanished like the smoke from his cigarette as it drifted upwards. He followed the blue swirl, his mind unable to see any way of finding his way back to the happiness he had known with Annie in the past.  And now, Lexie and Nancy were both out of his control and going, who knew where, with their lives.

He stubbed out his cigarette and drank the last of the tea.

Tomorrow was another day, he told himself and Annie would need him more than ever to bring back her happy smile. He looked at himself in the mirror over the sideboard, he was over 60 now and his once handsome face was showing the lines of age and the harshness of too many Scottish winters. And what had it all been for, he wondered, despite all his efforts, the fates seem to have won again.

Reassured that all was well, Lexie had managed to sleep and was ready for her trip to Montrose before Billy had woken.  She left a note for him and crept from the house before he could say anything that could prevent her from going and was soon boarding the Montrose bus again, her spirits rising with the dawn.

She tried to imagine what Wing Commander Martin Kettlewell would look like and if he'd think she was good enough to be his personal Secretary and if she'd be able to live on the Base or lodge in town, or if Winnie would be surprised… .anything rather than think how her mother was feeling.

It was daylight when the bus pulled into the bus station. Lexie alighted and set off towards the Base, she may have only been a few miles from Dundee, but for Lexie, she was going back to another world, the world she knew and loved, the RAF and that was a million miles away.

———oOo———

# Chapter 20

Billy Donnelly was waiting for his son in the Thrums Bar, nursing his second pint and thinking how he could use him to get back with Nancy.

"Hiya dad," wee Billy said, suddenly at his shoulder. Billy eyed his son and was taken aback by how mature he looked. At the start of the war, he'd been a child, but now he had taken on the outward signs of a man.

Billy turned to the bar tender. "Half of Shandy for the lad," he said, "and the same again for me."

The barman raised an eyebrow at wee Billy and made sure there was more lemonade than beer in his glass. He didn't need the polis on his back. Wee Billy didn't waste any time before asking his father when he was coming home. "I miss you, dad," he said, gazing at their reflections in the mirror over the bar "and so does everyone else...even mum."

Billy took a long draught of ale and wiped his mouth with the back of his hand. "And I miss you too, " he said, "but I don't think your mum's for me coming home. You see...." Billy began... ."I know," his son interrupted, "about Gladys Kelly and everything, but you just have to stop seeing her and mum will be fine." How simple it sounded to his young mind. "It's not as easy as you think," Billy said, changing the subject, quickly, away from Gladys Kelly. "Your Grandpa doesn't like me you see and he's turned your mum against me."

"Grandpa Dawson!" wee Billy exclaimed, "but what's he got to do with it?

Billy sighed, dramatically, "lets get out of here," he said, "you and me need to talk, man to man." Billy downed the last of his pint but wee Billy didn't touch his Shandy, much to the relief of the barman.

But it was more the man talked and the boy listened and by the time they'd walked from King Street to the Lochee Road, Billy had managed to paint a picture of himself as the victim and Billy Dawson as the bully who'd turned Nancy against him, even when he knew she went dancing with other men, while he was away fighting for his country. Gladys Kelly was only a friend, nothing more, but Billy Dawson had Nancy believing she was a Prostitute and that Billy was bedding her.

"So you see, son," he said, plaintively, "I want to come home, more than anything, but.....your mother....well, she won't have anything to do with me."

The Lochee tram rumbled into view.

"Will you meet me again?" Billy asked, hurriedly, shaking his son's hand like he was a man. "Same place next week?" he added "and maybe between the two of us, we can get your mum to see sense."

Wee Billy felt a tear forming as his father boarded the tram and watched as it clanged out of sight. One way or another, he had to make his mother see that Grandpa Dawson was the problem and not his dad. His dad wanted to come home and wee Billy was going to make sure it happened.

Billy smiled to himself as the tram made its way back to Gladys Kelly's single-end. He'd managed to talk his son onto his side and Nancy would have a hard job keeping him away, now that wee Billy wanted him to come home.

It had only gone 9 o'clock when Billy got back to Gladys's house and was surprised to find her in. She didn't usually come home from the Brothel before midnight, especially on a Friday night when the mill workers got their wages. But, one look at her ashen face, told him something was wrong. He pulled up a chair beside her.

"You're back early," he said, trying to keep his voice light, "Michael Flannaghan hasn't sacked you, has he?"

Gladys's chin began to quiver and wet tears started to run down her face. She shook her head and covered her mouth with a hankie.

Billy felt a frisson of concern and he pulled his chair closer.

"What is it?" he asked, "what's wrong?"

Gladys struggled to gain control of her emotions. "I've been to see a Doctor," she whispered, "and……." Harsh sobs wracked her body.

"Hey, hey," Billy said, worriedly, "don't take on so…..tell me what's wrong?"

Gladys turned bleak eyes on him. "He says I've got a bad disease," she said, "and I've to see somebody at the infirmary."

Billy felt a wave of panic wash over him. He knew only too well what 'a bad disease' was. They'd warned him about fraternising with the women in France and how they could pass 'bad diseases' onto the soldiers who were foolish enough to bed them.

Billy stood up and began pacing the floor, his fears multiplying with every step. What if Gladys had passed some horrible disease on to him, what if she had to stop working and the money she gave him would also stop, what if Michael Flannaghan had complaints from his punters and he came here and recognised him…..the list of his fears went on.

He reached for the bottle of rum Gladys kept on the sideboard and poured two shots, making it a double for himself.

"Drink this," he ordered Gladys, his hand shaking with fear that she had passed her 'bad disease' onto him already. "It's maybe not as bad as you think," he added unconvincingly, "let's wait and see what the Doctor at the hospital says." But Billy knew that before many more days had passed, he would have to leave Gladys and this place. His only hope now was that wee Billy could convince Nancy to give him another chance.

By the time wee Billy had returned home the hour was late and Nancy had been watching the clock, tick-tock away the minutes, her heart quickening at every sound on the landing since her son had left at

six o'clock. King Kevin was fast asleep and if Mary Anne noticed that her brother wasn't around, she said nothing and went off to bed at nine as usual.

Nancy tried to read wee Billy's face, but he was giving nothing away.

She waited till she could wait no more. "Well!" she said, finally, when he made no move to speak to her, "now do you believe me?"

Wee Billy shrugged. "Didn't say I didn't believe you," he said, evenly, "it's just that you've maybe been told something that wasn't true, that's all."

Nancy drew back. What had her husband been saying to their son?

"Meaning?" she asked, incredulously.

Wee Billy sat down facing her. "Meaning that what Grandpa's been telling you about dad, isn't true. Gladys Kelly's dad's friend, that's all."

Nancy felt a shock of disbelief rush through her head.

She knew her husband was a practiced liar, but surely, even he wouldn't lie to his own son.

"Is that what he told you?"

Wee Billy nodded, "he also told me about you out dancing and gallivanting with other men, while he was away at the war."

Nancy felt the colour drain from her face, unable to summon up words to explain herself.

"Well," her son said, "is that true or is it another of dad's lies."

Nancy's righteous indignation wilted, "it's true," she whispered into the silence, searching her son's eyes for understanding.

"Maybe you should speak to Grandpa then," he said over his shoulder, as he headed to the back room, "find out for yourself whether dad's telling the truth or not."

Nancy felt the shame of her past when she'd let Jim Murphy into her bed, believing that her husband was unfaithful. She still didn't know how Billy had found out and to tell wee Billy about it was unforgiveable. But even as she thought it, she realised that she had told their son that his father was bedding a Prostitute. Somehow, Billy had managed to put her in the wrong in her son's eyes and there wasn't a thing she could do about it.

Slowly she damped down the fire and turned the gas mantle low, before crawling into her bed and pulling the covers over her head to muffle the sounds of her hurt. Maybe things would look better in the morning, but she doubted it. She'd be starting back to work next Monday, but till then, she had to speak to her father, find out the truth.

But Billy Dawson had problems of his own to deal with, Lexie had gone to Montrose for her interview but he had to get Dr McFarlane to visit Annie and find out what was wrong with her.

He telephoned the Doctor and arranged to meet him at Isabella's house at 11 o'clock that morning, before telephoning Isabella to ask how Annie was faring.

"Not well," she'd told him, she's had a little breakfast, but still doesn't seem to want to do anything but sleep.

"I'll be right over," Billy said "and Dr McFarlane's coming at eleven."

The Doctor arrived exactly on time and once he'd taken off his coat and hat and looked at Annie over his half-moon spectacles, he ushered Isabella and Billy out of the room.

"Now then, Annie Dawson, he said, more to himself than his patient, "what have we here."

He checked her pulse, took her temperature, listened to her heart and lungs with his stethoscope and checked her for any lumps and bumps, before sitting back and smiling at the reclining figure.

"Can't find anything physically wrong with you, Mrs Dawson," he said, gently, "so maybe you should tell me what's troubling you, eh?"

As usual, when faced with kindness, Annie became tearful and all the strain of the losses that she'd had to face over the years came pouring out. Dr McFarlane listened, without interrupting, till Annie came up to date with the loss of Lexie, not to illness or death, but to RAF Montrose.

The Doctor patted her hand. "I think that man of yours needs to take you on a wee holiday," he said, "get some colour back in those cheeks."

Despite herself, Annie began to smile. "Yes, Doctor," she said, "I think maybe you're right."

"She's what we call depressed," Dr McFarlane told Billy, while Isabella scuttled back to Annie with a cup of tea. "She's had a hard time of it all her life and it's just caught up with her a bit."

"So, she's not got a disease or anything like that?" Billy asked, anxiously, remembering how Annie's siste, Mary, had died from Tuberculosis."

"Nothing like that," the Doctor reassured him, "but I do think a change of scenery won't go amiss, you know what they say, a change is as good as a rest."

Billy thanked the Doctor and paid him his fee. "I think I know just the place to take her," he said and I'll make arrangements right away."

Billy went back into the room and asked Isabella for a minute alone with Annie. "Of course," Isabella said, "I'll be in the kitchen if you need anything else," she told Annie.

Billy took her hand and kissed her on the lips. "I think it's time Annie Pepper," he said, smiling, "that we go to Belfast and visit our son."

Annie felt a rush of energy force its way into her body at the thought of seeing her first-born son again. He had followed in the footsteps of his adopted father, Dr John Adams and was qualified now himself as a specialist 'baby doctor', working at Belfast Infirmary.

"Do you really mean it?" Annie said, her eyes beginning to shine and a blush of colour returning to her cheeks.

"Of course, I mean it," Billy reassured her, "and if you like, we could be there for Christmas."

Annie threw her arms around Billy. "God isn't punishing me after all" she whispered, "he still loves me."

Billy held her tighter, wondering how long Annie had believed that, somehow, God was punishing her and for doing nothing more than loving him and giving birth to his son. Not for the first time, he realised how much people feared the Lord, or maybe it was the priests and ministers who spoke on His behalf, that they feared.

"Everything is fine," he told her, "with you, me and God Almighty, now, let's get home and start packing."

—-—oOo—-—

# Chapter 21

Lexie approached the gate into the Base, her heart thumping and her throat dry.  One of the guards stopped her, asking her business, before checking his list and allowing her to enter.

Wing Commander Martin Kettlewell was studying a map on the wall behind his desk when Lexie was shown in.

"Miss Melville," the WAAF announced, before ushering Lexie into the Wing Commander's Office.  Martin Kettlewell turned to face her.

"Miss Melville," he smiled, "welcome to RAF Montrose." He indicated a seat and Lexie sat on the edge of it.  He opened a drawer and removed a buff folder from it.  "Wing Commander Johnson sent me your records," he said, "and I must say, they're quite a read."  He flicked through the pages, settling on the letter from the Government awarding Lexie her Empire Medal. "Congratulations on your medal," he said "and there's no doubting your bravery and loyalty to the service," he added, before giving Lexie his full attention, "but I wonder if working as a civilian at the base will be enough for you?"

For a moment Lexie couldn't speak.  She was counting on this job as the Wing Commander's secretary so much, she'd never given it a thought that she would be seen as almost over-qualified by the Empire Medal!

"But...........that was what anyone would have done," she stammered, "and now the war's over......I just want to do something useful......and it seemed with my time in the WAAF, I would be......."

Martin Kettlewell held up his hand to stop her.  "It's alright," he said, "Wing Commander Johnson wouldn't have recommended you so highly if he didn't think you could cope with the job, but what I need to know is that you'll be able to do the work as a 'civilian' and not hanker for being back in the Service?"

In an instant Lexie was forced to consider why she wanted to work at the RAF Base, after all, she could just as easily be a secretary at Baxters Office in Dundee, in fact, she would be more than that, she would be the Office Manager! Had Martin Kettlewell hit at the heart of her need to keep in touch with her WAAF life or was she just trying to escape from a future in Dundee.

For her own sake, Lexie had to be sure before she answered. Going back to her life in Dundee wasn't an option and, whatever her future held, it had to start again where her life had stopped, when she was demobbed from the Air Force.

Lexie straightened her back. Once before, at the recruitment office in Dundee she'd been asked her reason for wanting to enlist in the WAAF and now she was being asked again about her commitment, by Martin Kettlewell.

"Because I want to use my skills as a secretary and my understanding of the Air Force procedures to support you as Wing Commander at RAF Montrose," Lexie stated firmly and with conviction.

Martin Kettlewell considered her answer. Johnny Johnson had told him of Lexie's involvement with the Canadian Air Force Captain, Bo McGhee and the untimely death of the man she'd married, Captain Robertson, in a torpedo hit at sea, but he had to be sure the girl in front of him was emotionally able to be his confidante as well as his secretary. The war may be over, but covert work would still go on. Her awarding of the Empire Medal had convinced him that she had what it took to deal with wartime and her professional answer now reassured him that Lexie could also cope with anything peacetime might throw at her.

"When can you start?" he said, his eyes registering the relief in Lexie's own.

"The job's mine?" she whispered, all of the tension of the past weeks flowing out of her system.

Wing Commander Kettlewell stood up and extended a hand. "Monday, suit you?"

Lexie nodded vigorously.  "Monday will be just fine," she said… "and thank you."

His handshake was warm and reassuring and Lexie now knew for certain, that whatever the future held, right now, she'd made the right decision. She wasn't going back to Dundee, she was going forward to Montrose.

By the time Lexie had told her good news to Winnie and travelled back to Dundee, her spirits were soaring, but as she got nearer to home, misgivings about her mother's strange 'illness' were beginning to form.

"It's only me," she called as she came into the lobby, "anyone home?"

Billy's head popped round the kitchen door.  "In here," he signalled to Lexie, "your mum's asleep and we need to have a wee chat."

Lexie took off her coat and hung it on the Hallstand, a bit perplexed at Billy's suggestion of a 'wee chat.'

"Is everything alright?" she asked as Billy poured her some tea before topping up his own cup.

"She's fine," he assured her, she's just got a bit low that's all. The Doctor says it's nothing to worry about, but how about you, how did things go at Montrose?"

Lexie was aware of Billy changing the subject on to her, but she wanted to tell him her news before she had to confront her mother again.

"I got the job," she said, "starting Monday."

"Well!" Billy exclaimed, "that's wonderful."

Lexie was a bit taken aback at Billy's response, considering her mother's reaction to her leaving again had caused her so much upset.  He could see her perplexed expression and smiled. "You're not the only one who's leaving home," he said excitedly, "your mother and me are off to Belfast to see our son, John, for Christmas." Billy wanted to add that they wouldn't be returning to Dundee, but he had to convince Annie of that before saying any more. Annie's depression and Lexie's departure to Montrose had shown him how little was left for either of them in Dundee and the prospect of living out the rest of their lives in Ireland and being close to their son was almost too good to be true.

Lexie almost dropped her cup. All of a sudden, 'the boot was on the other foot' and it was she who felt left behind. Her half-brother had been in the background for years, but this announcement had brought him back into her life with a bang!

"So, mum won't be here for Christmas?" Lexie asked, sadly.

Billy eyed her quizzically. "Is that a problem?" he said, "seeing as how you won't be here for Christmas either."

"That's not the point," she said, "mum's always here at Christmas," she added lamely. Venturing out into the world alone was one thing, but not having her mother to come home to if it all went wrong, was quite another.

Billy lit a cigarette and watched Lexie's eyes cloud over.

"You can't have it both ways Lexie," he said kindly, "and freedom can be a lonely place."

The sound of the kitchen door opening alerted Lexie and Billy to Annie's entering. Billy immediately went towards her, wondering how much of their conversation she'd heard. He didn't have long to wait to find out.

"Lexie! Annie exclaimed, sitting down at the table next to Billy, "how was the trip to Montrose?"

Lexie hesitated, while Billy poured Annie some tea. Her mother did look a bit pale, but otherwise, seemed well enough to hear her news.

"I got the job," she said avoiding eye contact with her mother, "Secretary to Wing Commander Martin Kettlewell, starting on Monday."

There, it was out. She looked up at a smiling Annie, relieved that her news seemed to have been well received, but strangely deflated at her mother's ready acceptance of her going this time.

"Has Billy told you our news?" Annie asked.

"About going to Belfast?" Lexie countered, glancing at Billy.

"Yes he has."

"So, we won't be here for Christmas," Annie said " nor for the New Year, for that matter," she added, smiling at her husband. Billy nodded his agreement. He was now sure Annie had heard Lexie's words, but it seemed that she had decided that Lexie was no longer her little girl and was saying that they both had to accept that mother and daughter would now be going their separate ways.

Lexie suddenly wanted to rush over to her mother, wrap her arms around her and tell her how much she loved her, as a deep feeling of rejection flowed through her. But it was all too late, the die was cast and everything she'd wanted was now happening, she would be leaving home but, so too, would her mother. Whether she liked it or not, there was no way back and in that moment, Lexie became a woman, alone in the world she had created.

—·—oOo—·—

# Chapter 22

Nancy handed the sleepy Kevin over to Isabella at the Salvation Army Hall, along with the rest of the early-morning mums depositing their bairns to be minded, before hurrying off to work at the jute mills.

"I can't thank you enough," she said to Isabella, who'd readily agreed to look after the infant so that Nancy could get back to the weaving at Baxters. Billy Donnelly had been 'bad news' ever since Nancy had taken up with him, getting her pregnant before, eventually, marrying her.

And now, she was on her own again, thanks to his philandering with Gladys Kelly. Unforgiveable, Isabella had decided, her Christian values not being able to overlook Billy's behaviour.

"I'll be back for him at six," Nancy said, re-fastening her coat and pulling the knotted turban over her cold ears. Isabella waved her off and set Kevin down on his feet. "C'mon, little man," she cooed, "let's get you some warm milk and see who we can find for you to play with. Isabella gazed at the child as he drank the milk, he was a bonny wee bairn that was for sure, but she wondered what the future might hold for him without a dad and with a working mum who would no longer be at home.

Nancy hurried down William Lane's steps leading to Baxters and was the first into the Weaving Flat.

John Brannan looked up as she came in and smiled at her. Someone's keen, he thought, admiring again Nancy's trim figure and dark hair peeping out from under her turban as she came over to his desk.

"Reporting for duty," she said, her eyes sparkling. She'd done it, she told herself as she breathed in the smell of the jute and all by herself. She didn't need Billy Donnelly, in fact, she didn't need anyone, from now on, she would live the life she wanted and wasn't answerable to anyone, even wee Billy.

"You look pleased with yourself," John said, pointing towards a pair of looms, waiting to be set on, "hope you're still as cheery by knocking-off time."

Nancy grinned. "I'll be even cheerier when I get my wages on Friday," she quipped, already feeling as if she'd never been away from the mill and the years between had almost never happened.

She started up her looms along with the rest of the weavers. Very quickly, the racket drowned out any hope of chatting and it was only when the 'bummer' sounded for dinner-time, that there was a chance of renewing her acquaintance with the other women.

The canteen was spartan, with green painted walls and wooden tables and a cook who only seemed to manage to make soup and mince.

There were nudges from Nancy's co-workers as she came in and found a vacant table to set down her tray of soup and bread.

The word had got round fast, as the gossip about Nancy and her 'carry on' with Jim Murphy, became the topic of conversation. The Supervisor had been sacked by Mr Dawson and Jim Murphy's wife had made sure everyone knew that Nancy was to blame for all her marital woes. The hussy!

"And her man's left her for anither wuman" Wilma Small advised, knowingly "and wha could blame'im." Arms and legs were added by whisperer after whisperer, till Nancy was painted as a harlot and man-eater and that John Brannan, Jim Murphy's replacement, had better watch out or she'd have her claws into him.

The gossip heightened to fever pitch, when John Brannan joined Nancy at her table and all eyes were watching as he sat down.

John looked around the canteen, where tables of women were suddenly very interested in their plates, as he stared them out.

"Looks like you could use a friend," he said, drawing Nancy's attention to her workmates avoiding eyes.

Nancy felt a rush of colour to her face. She might have known that the gossip mongers would have a field day, but it still hurt that not one of the women seemed willing to defend her. Even Di Auchterlonie, had kept her distance, a women Nancy had felt understood why she'd turned to another man for love.


Her eyes levelled with John Brannan. "I suppose you're wondering what it's all about," she said, not really knowing why she wanted to tell him anything, but aware that, pretty soon, he might be the only friend she had at the mill.

"Not really," John said, quietly, "I'm more wondering why you let crones like that bother you." He nodded to the tables of women. "Have you considered that they might just be jealous?"

Nancy shook her head and pushed aside the now cold soup, her day that had started with so much hope and joy, had quickly deteriorated to hopelessness. "I need some fresh air," she said, standing up and turning to face her accusers, "there's a bad smell in here," she added, loudly, before walking out of the canteen, her head held high.

John Brannan watched Nancy till she disappeared through the door. This woman was not just beautiful, she was fearless and one way or another, he was determined to get closer to her. He pushed all thoughts of her past from his mind, whatever had happened, he would deal with it. He was now, more sure than ever, that he wanted Nancy Donnelly in his life.

By the time her shift was finished and she'd picked up King Kevin, Nancy wanted nothing more than to sit down and fall asleep, but there was food to prepare for her brood and a pile of ironing to get through before she could relax. She struggled up the stone stairs of the tenement and was relieved to see that there was light shining from the kitchen window. Hoping that Mary Anne was already home from work and would, at least, have some tea ready, she pushed open the door.

But it wasn't Mary Anne she saw, it was wee Billy and sitting across from him, was the gaunt figure of Billy Donnelly, looking sheepish and sorry for himself, but she'd seen that look before.

"Dad's got nowhere to go!" wee Billy exclaimed, hurriedly, glancing at his father for support. Billy Donnelly said nothing.

Nancy felt a surge of white-hot anger flow through her veins.

"GET OUT," she screamed, pulling her husband to his feet with a strength that came from nowhere, "AND DON'T EVER COME BACK."

Billy knew Nancy meant business and now wasn't the time to try to win her back. "I'm sorry," he said, "wee Billy thought....."

"GET OUT," Nancy shouted again, her heart hammering and her eyes blazing.

"Sorry son," he murmured to wee Billy, who stood rooted to the spot with fear. He'd never seen his mother so angry and knew now, that if he wanted to see his dad again, it would have to be in secret and without his mother's approval and the child in him silently wept.


Wee Billy ran through to the back room before his mother could see his tears, as King Kevin tugged at Nancy's skirt. "Me hungry," he said, looking up at his mum with wide-eyed innocence. Nancy lifted him up and walked him over to the biscuit barrel where she picked out a Custard Cream, which Kevin promptly bit into. Just then, Nancy heard the door open again and a feeling of dread filled her soul, surely Billy wouldn't be coming back again, but it was Mary Anne and Nancy breathed a sigh of relief.

"Did I just see dad coming out of the close?" she asked, surprise and happiness in her face. Nancy set Kevin back on his feet. She was going to have to talk things out with wee Billy and Mary Anne, but not now, right now, she was feeling washed out and exhausted.

"Help me with the tea," she said to her daughter, wearily, "and I'll explain everything later."

Billy Donnelly hurried down William Lane and into King Street. His hands were frozen along with his heart. If he thought getting back with Nancy was going to be easy, he now knew he was wrong. Whatever had happened to his wife while he'd been at war, it had turned her into a force to be reckoned with. Long gone was the compliant, needy woman he had married.

The lights of the Thrums Bar beckoned him in. He didn't want to go back to Gladys and her 'bad' disease, he didn't want to even think about that and what it might mean. Right now, he just wanted to blot out the encounter with Nancy and get drunk.

"Pint of heavy and a nip o' Bells," he told the barman, "and no short measures."

The barman raised his eyebrows. Someone was in a bad mood, he thought, which didn't bode well as the evening was still young and a man could drink a fair amount of whiskey before closing time.

"No short measures in the Thrums," the barman assured Billy, briskly, pushing the glass under the upturned bottle of Bell's Whisky on the optic, but before he could begin pulling the pint of beer, Billy had downed the drink and asked for another.

The bar wasn't busy on a Monday night and the barman was glad when another customer came through the swinging door. He had a feeling that trouble was brewing and he didn't want to be alone if it did.

"I'll be with you in a minute Mr Brannan," he said, indicating the slowly filling pint glass.

"No hurry, Pat," John said, "finish serving the man." He looked at Billy, who had drunk the second whiskey and was now staring at the pint of beer that had been placed in front of him.

Pat indicated, with a nervous glance, that the drinker at the end of the bar might be a problem and John Brannan nodded. He'd seen it all before, he'd been a Sergeant in the Scots Guards during the war and he knew how to handle drunks. But the war was over now and many a soldier had come home to find he no longer fitted in with civilian life and turned to drink to take the edge of his loneliness.

"Cold night out," he said easily, addressing the words to Billy, while waiting for his pint to be delivered. The barman's eyes remained fixed on his task.  Billy looked at the man.  "Aye."

"The name's Brannan," John said, extending his hand, "John Brannan."

Billy shook his hand, "Donnelly," he replied, "Billy Donnelly," while wondering if the newcomer might stand him a drink.

The barman breathed a sigh of relief.  There would be no fighting tonight.

John drank an inch of beer.  Had he just introduced himself to Nancy Donnelly's husband?

"Escaping from the wife?" John asked, pointing to the rapidly reducing pint in front of Billy.

"What's it to you?" Billy retorted, ordering another Bell's.

"Sorry," John said, apologetically, "didn't mean to be nosey. Here, let me get this one."

He pushed half a crown towards Pat "and have one for yourself barman," he added, "I had a win on the ponies on Saturday, so I'm a bit flush."

The atmosphere eased and another whiskey was placed in front of Billy.

"Cheers," John said, raising his glass, "here's to a peaceful Christmas." "I'll drink to that an' all," Pat said, "but after closing time'" he added, tapping the side of his nose and winking.  He knew better than to join in with the drinkers when he was on duty and turned his hand to polishing the tumblers behind the bar instead.

Billy made short work of the third whiskey, but said nothing.

"Not looking forward to Christmas then?" John asked. By this time, the effects of the alcohol were bringing out the anger in Billy.  He was angry at Gladys for being so stupid as to get infected with Syphilis and forcing him back out onto the streets, he was angry at Billy Dawson for telling Nancy about his visits to the prostitute, but most of all, he was angry at Nancy for telling him to get out of her life. Trying to get back through using wee Billy hadn't worked and now that Nancy was back at the weaving, she didn't need him for anything anymore.

He slammed down the empty whiskey glass and gulped down the last of the beer.

"Happy bloody Christmas," he spat, as he headed unsteadily to the pub door, knocking against John Brannan as he did so, spilling his drink.

John grabbed his arm and steadied him. "I think you need to go home," he said, "get your wife to feed you."

Billy shook himself free, his eyes black with temper. "What wife," he shouted, "Nancy bloody Donnelly's no wife of mine anymore."

"That's been coming a long time," Pat said, as the pub door swung shut behind Billy, "he's been at it with some prostitute in Lochee for years now, but wanted to have his cake and eat it, till his wife kicked him out."

So that was it in a nutshell. "Where does he live then?" John asked.

The barman shrugged his shoulders, "used to live on the Viccy Road, but that was before, you know...."

John finished the last of his pint. "Better be getting home myself," he said, "an early start the morn." But John Brannan didn't turn towards the Cowgate, instead he turned towards the disappearing figure of Billy Donnelly, who had just turned up William Lane. John quickly realised he was going towards Victoria Road and Nancy, and God knows what state he'd be in when he got there.

There were no lights at the window of Nancy's kitchen when Billy stumbled to her door.

"Open up!" He yelled. "It's your man, home from the war."

Nancy sat bolt upright in her bed, a real fear gripping her shivering body. She knew Billy well and had experienced his out-of-control temper before, when he'd found out about Jim Murphy and tried to throttle her.

She threw back the bedcovers and ran through to the back room to waken wee Billy and Mary Anne, but they were awake already.

"What's happening?" Mary Anne asked her mother, her eyes wide with confusion.

"It's dad, isn't it" wee Billy said, shakily.

"Thanks to you," Nancy said harshly, wishing instantly she

could take back the words she had spoken. It wasn't her son's fault.

The sound of Billy banging on the door increased.

"HE'S BREAKING IN!" Nancy's voice was rising with anxiety, as she heard the lock burst and the front door bang against the wall.

Billy pushed the door to the back room open, there was no going back for him now, if he couldn't have Nancy, then no one could.

"WHORE" he shouted, as wee Billy and Mary Anne, backed away from him and Kevin, wakened by the noise, began screaming.

Nancy shook from head to foot. She couldn't stand up to her husband when he was sober, let alone drunk and she knew it.

"GET AWAY FROM ME," she tried to say, but the words were smothered by fear, as Billy drew closer. Any love there had been between them was gone forever as he back-handed Nancy across her face.

Wee Billy jumped to her defence, but was swatted aside like an annoying bluebottle. He turned his attention back to his wife and was about to slap her again, when a pair of strong hands clamped onto his shoulders and dragged him backwards.

He struggled to turn around to see who was behind him, but couldn't release himself from the iron grip. Once they were onto the landing, Billy felt the force of an uppercut punch knock him on his back. The same hands picked him up again, this time sinking a punch into his stomach.

Billy folded over and staggered backwards, till a final punch to his jaw sent him reeling against the railings.

Blood was pouring from his mouth and vomit was racing up into his throat, as he tried to focus his eyes on his assailant.

John Brannan pulled Billy towards him. "You heard Mrs Donnelly," he said, almost politely, "don't come back here, because if you do, I'll be waiting." He shoved Billy towards the stairs and watched, as he staggered down them, back into the night.

John Brannan knocked on the broken front door. Nancy was cuddling Kevin in her arms as wee Billy and Mary Anne cowered behind her.

"Who is it?" Nancy called out and to her amazement, John Brannan walked into the kitchen.

"Mr Brannan," she said in disbelief, "but how….."

John held up his hand.  "I was in the Thrums," he said, "and your man was getting the worse for drink.  When the barman said who he was, I thought I'd better follow him and make sure you came to no harm."

He looked at the broken door and the frightened family. "Just as well I did," he said "and I don't think he'll be bothering you again."

"I don't know how to thank you," Nancy said, her heart rate returning to normal.

"No thanks needed," John said, "but if he's any more trouble…..let me know."

Nancy nodded, numbly.

"See you tomorrow," John said, turning to go, "and if you're a little late, I'll understand.  You've had quite a fright."

"Who was that?" Mary Anne asked tentatively, when their 'saviour' had gone.  Nancy sighed.  "I'll tell you tomorrow," she said, exhaustion washing over her again, "but right now, let's get some sleep."

Without being asked, wee Billy tried to set the door back into place and braced it with a chair.  This was a side of his father he'd never seen before and it scared him.

"Goodnight mum," he said, his young eyes bleak and tearful.

"Goodnight son," Nancy replied, "see you in the morning."

——-—oOo——-—

# Chapter 23

Lexie had intended taking the bus back to Montrose, lugging her case of belongings with her.  But, Billy would have none of it. "Your mother and me will take you in the motor car," he said, as they ate their Sunday breakfast, "make sure you get settled into your lodgings before the big day."

She would have preferred to just 'go' but the offer of a lift in the motor would make things easier, especially as the grip of winter was tightening and the sky was heavy with snow clouds.

She had expected her mother to break down as they neared Montrose, but Annie seemed almost buoyant and it was Lexie who had to steel herself to say a final goodbye.

"You have the telephone number," Billy said, as he hefted her case from the boot of the motorcar, we'll be at home till the first week in December, then.....well...we'll contact you by letter from Belfast."

Lexie nodded, tight-lipped, wondering if she'd ever see her mother again and beginning to hate herself for being so determined to leave Dundee.  Why couldn't she just have let things be and go back to work at Baxters and live at home.....but even as she thought it, she knew it wouldn't have worked for long.

"Fine," she said instead "and thanks for the lift."


Her mother wound down the window at the passenger side and reached out a gloved hand. "We'll give John your love," she said, still buoyant and happy, "and remember to telephone if......well, you won't need to."

A blown kiss and the motorcar window closed.  Lexie had never felt so alone in her life as she watched the motor pull away and head back to Dundee.

But Bertha Adams was watching Lexie's arrival from the window and her   heart went out to the young girl.  Along with her husband, Jock, they'd agreed to her lodging with them, if she got the job at the base. As Winnie's best friend from their days in the WAAF, it seemed a perfect way for the girls to be company for one another and it also provided Jock and Bertha with a steady income from the rent of the room.

"Come away in," she called to Lexie, beckoning to her from the front door, "you'll freeze to death on that pavement."

Lexie took a deep breath and turned to face Winnie's mum. "Just coming," she said, painting on a smile she didn't feel.  This was what I wanted, she reminded herself, and tomorrow she would start work as Wing Commander Martin Kettlewell's private secretary.  There was no turning back and that was the end of it.

Winnie was bouncing with excitement when she came home from work at the base to find Lexie having a cup of tea in the kitchen.

"You got the job!" she squealed, "I knew you would."

The two girls hugged, while Jock and Bertha smiled to themselves.  Winnie had told them about the death of Lexie's husband, Robbie Robertson and they had been more than happy to agree with Winnie's asking that Lexie stay with them if she came to work at the Base.

Winnie's enthusiasm was infectious and Lexie's mood brightened as she helped her unpack her few belongings in her new room.

"It's not much," Winnie said, "but it's home until you find your feet."

"It's lovely," Lexie replied "and once I've had a good night's sleep, I'll be ready to face whatever life throws at me."

"Good," said Winnie, reluctantly taking the hint and leaving Lexie to get some rest, "see you at breakfast," she grinned, "then it'll be full steam ahead to the base."

The door closed quietly and Lexie lay down on the single bed and closed her eyes.  Images of her mother waving her goodbye mixed with her wedding day to Robbie and the telegram telling her he'd been killed filled her heart. A tear threatened to escape from her eyes at the sadness of it all, fate had managed to turn a full circle in Lexie's life and now she felt back where she had begun when she'd first left Dundee to join the WAAF, alone and scared.

She pushed herself up on her elbows and swung her feet back onto the floor and rummaging in her open suitcase, she unearthed a large, brown envelope.

Inside was the paper-story of her life. There were photos of her family, her marriage lines and Robbie's death certificate, a few letters and cards, the velvet pouch holding her Empire Medal and her discharge papers. The war was over and everything she looked at was the past and her future was yet to be seen. Lexie felt a shiver of the unknown run through her. Had she made the right decision to face the world alone?

Hurriedly, she pushed everything back into the envelope and clicked the suitcase closed. Tomorrow, a new chapter of her life would begin.

Wing Commander Martin Kettlewell had spent his Sunday in his Quarters catching up on personal correspondence. He'd written to his friend, Wing Commander Johnny Johnson, telling him of Lexie's interview and thanking him for sending her to RAF Montrose and now he had one more letter to write. He took out a fresh sheet of airmail writing paper and began,

*Dear Bo*
*Lexie's here at Montrose and she will be working for me as my Private Secretary as from tomorrow. She turned up at Lossiemouth asking Johnny Johnson for a job at the base and he got in touch with me, to see if I could offer her work. Of course I said I could.*
*Let me know what you want me to do.*
*Uncle Martin*

Martin Kettlewell addressed the envelope.

Wing Commander R McGhee,
Canadian Royal Airforce
CRAF Base Moose Jaw,
Saskatchuan,
Canada.

Martin sealed the letter, he'd post it tomorrow.  Bo had survived the war but his marriage hadn't.  He'd married a flirtatious girl, Angela Lafeyette, from Quebec on the rebound of Lexie's rejection and had regretted it almost immediately. Martin didn't blame Angela for leaving Bo, the marriage was never going to work, everyone knew that, but she'd also left their son with Bo to bring up alone.

Martin shook his head. It would take a miracle for his nephew to find happiness again and a very special woman to also accept Bo and Angela's son.  He lit a cigarette and watched the smoke curl into the air, wondering if Lexie was that girl and whether she still felt anything for Bo, the man who'd never stopped loving her.

Nancy felt shaken and exhausted as she tried to make some breakfast for her brood.  Her husband's visit the night before had made her realise how vulnerable she was to another visit and determined that now she was earning money again, she would have to think of finding somewhere else to live for her own safety and that of her family, especially wee Billy, who'd seen his father at his worst and it had frightened him quite badly.

Almost instinctively, her mind raced to her father, he'd offered her a cottage in the Stannergate, before Billy's behaviour had smashed any chance of continuing with their marriage, maybe the offer was still open.

Nancy didn't have long to find out.

"Nancy," she heard her father's voice calling, anxiously, from behind the broken door, "it's dad, let me in."

Nancy rushed to remove the chair wee Billy had set against the door preventing it from being pushed open and her father rushed in. His eyes ranged over the bairns who looked white and shaken, but otherwise unhurt, his eyes finally resting on his daughter.

"What happened?" he asked, holding Nancy by the shoulders and focussing all his attention on her words.

"Billy broke in last night," she told him, "he was mad with drink and.....oh! dad," she said, "he's not in control of himself anymore."

"Hush now, Nancy," Billy Dawson said, wrapping his arms around her and signalling to Mary Anne to make some tea.

"He was like a wild man, Grandpa," wee Billy said, his eyes still wide with fear, "I hate him!" he added vehemently.

"He won't be back," Billy said, steadily you can be sure of that and the best thing you can do is get to your work and let me and your mother sort this mess out. "You too, Mary Anne," he continued, "everything will be alright by the time you finish your shift."

Mary Anne set the teapot of fresh tea on the table and nodded to wee Billy that they should go. "Here," Nancy said, handing each of them a bread roll spread with margarine and jam, "this will keep you going till dinnertime."

The two of them inched out around the broken door and Nancy felt her trembling diminish as she poured the tea and gave Kevin some porridge and milk.

"How did you know something was wrong?" she asked her father.

"John Brannan," Billy said, "telephoned me from the Mill."

Nancy nodded. "It was lucky he was at the Thrums and knew Billy was trouble, but I might not be so lucky the next time....." her eyes began to darken with worry, "we're not safe here," she said, "not anymore."

Nancy didn't know that her father and Annie were heading for Belfast for Christmas, but before they went he was determined Nancy and her family would move from this house to somewhere safe.

Billy drank his tea and considered the possibilities open to Nancy.

"The cottage at the Stannergate isn't for rent anymore," he said.  Nancy felt her heart sink, she'd been counting on the refuge still being available, "but there may be a house in the Cowgate I can get my hands on.  Big enough for all of you and behind the East Port Mill, so you would be near help if you needed it."

Nancy couldn't believe her ears.  "Truly," she said, a rush of energy returning to her body.

"Leave it with me," Billy said, "I'll make a couple of telephone calls," he nodded, reassuringly, "and I'll send someone up from the Mill to fix that door."

"What would I do without you," Nancy gushed, throwing her arms around her father's neck."

"I thought you didn't need men in your life," Billy smiled, benignly.

Nancy felt her face redden and her eyes blinked downwards. Her father was right, she maybe didn't need Billy Donnelly in her life anymore, but coping in the world without a man was not going to be as easy as she had first thought.

For Billy Donnelly, life couldn't have gotten any worse. Gladys did have Syphilis, making her not only untouchable but meaning his main source of income had also dried up.  He nursed his swollen lip, glad of the icy air around him and hurried to his mother's house, she at least, would be glad to see him.  But the door had been boarded up. Clumsy planks of wood had been hammered across the frame making it impossible to get in.

He pounded loudly on a neighbour's door, panic beginning to grip his mind. "Where's Mrs Donnelly," he shouted through the letterbox, "its Billy," he added, "where's my ma?"

The single word reply knocked the stuffing out of him. "DEAD."

Billy's legs gave way and he slid down the wall, sobs of self-pity beginning to rack his body.  All the women in his life, who he'd abused and used were gone from him, even his mother couldn't save him now.

He didn't know how long he sat on the stone slabs of the

close floor, but it was pitch dark when he eventually made his choice and tomorrow, he would carry it out.

# Chapter 24

Lexie hardly slept and by five o'clock on the Monday morning, she was tiptoeing around the tiny room, selecting what to wear for her first day as Wing Commander Kettlewell's private secretary and polishing her shoes to the required 'regimental' shine.

Her nerves were jangling as she squinted at the small face of the watch on her wrist, so much hinged on getting everything just right. She had to be faultless in everything she did, she told herself, lest the Wing Commander saw through her front of bravado and  dismissed her as incompetent.  The shame of having to go back to Dundee with her 'tail between her legs' and ask Billy for her old job back, was just too awful to contemplate.

The sound of a knock on her room door, forced her to stop the train of scary thoughts that were chugging round her brain. "It's open," she called and Winnie's smiling face came into view. "Breakfast's ready," she said, "can't go to your new job on an empty stomach," she quipped.

The last thing Lexie felt like doing was eating, but she followed Winnie to the kitchen where Bertha Adams was spooning scrambled eggs onto toast.

"Come away in Lexie," she smiled, "this'll set you up for the day."

Despite her knotted stomach, Lexie managed to eat the eggs and helped Winnie clear the table before the two girls set off to the base.

The Winter morning was still dark, but the moon and occasional street lamp had turned the snow-covered world into a glittering wonderland. Lexie breathed in the cold air and felt herself relax a little.  Everything was going to be alright, she told herself, determinedly and by Christmas she would, hopefully, be settled into her new routine.

"We're nearly there," Winnie said quietly, picking up on Lexie's nerves.

Lexie nodded and smiled at her friend, "and everything will be alright," Winnie added, reassuringly.

The airman on guard checked their identification and signalled them through and before Lexie had any more time to think, she was into the Reception Office and knocking on the Wing Commander's door.

Lexie's nerves quickly disappeared as she tackled the pile of paperwork awaiting her, tried out the new typewriter and got to grips with the filing system in her little side room connected to Martin Kettlewell's Office and before she knew it, it was four o'clock and the Wing Commander asked her to come through and to bring her notebook.

Lexie hurried through and took her seat at the other side of the desk, her anxiety beginning to rise again. This was the moment when she would either be accepted or rejected. Had she done enough?

Martin Kettlewell was quick to assure Lexie that he was pleased with her work ethic. "In fact" he said, "I think I'm going to find it hard to keep up with you."

A wide grin of relief spread over her face. "Thank you, sir," he said, "I'll do my best to make sure....."

Martin held up a stopping hand. "Everything's fine," he said, "so slow down and enjoy the work, you're going to be here for a long time."

Reassured, Lexie stopped speaking and awaited her next instruction.

For the next two hours, boss and secretary worked through the many items of correspondence, including papers marked "Top Secret" and the list of future meetings and visitors to the base and it was dark again outside before Martin Kettlewell called a halt.

"I think that's more than enough for your first day," he said, "and well done."

Lexie was beaming as she gathered up the various documents and returned to her room. Martin Kettlewell watched her go. She'd more than lived up to his expectation as a worker and he could see the flashes of humour and sparkle that Bo would have been attracted to. But, how would she react when she knew he was Bo's uncle and that he was reporting back to him about her.

Lexie ran and skipped through the snow back to Winnie's parents' house, her happiness at impressing the Wing Commander bubbling up

as she came through the front door.

Bertha and Winnie exchanged glances and smiled. "Had a good day?" Bertha asked. "WONDERFUL" Lexie replied, "JUST WONDERFUL."

Everyone laughed at Lexie's enthusiasm. "So, you think you'll go back tomorrow?" Jock Adams asked, joining in the fun.

Lexie looked at the smiling family around her, her eyes sparkling with happiness, "tomorrow and forever," she said, "so, you'd best get used to me being around."

That night, Lexie slept like a log, all worries about her decision to face the world alone had vanished and she would write to her mother the following day and wish her and Billy every happiness when they were reunited with John in Belfast. She was sure now she'd never be going back to her old life in Dundee.

Billy Dawson did as he had said he would to Nancy and telephoned his Masonic friend when he got back to the Mill, about the chance of renting one of his houses to her in the Cowgate. The factor, Stanley Shepherd was as good as gold and assured Billy that as soon as she was able Nancy should come down to his office and arrange to pick up the key of number 16 Cowgate.

"Many thanks, Stanley," Billy said, "that's one I owe you."

"Pleasure," Stanley replied, "see you at the next meeting."

A Joiner was sent to fix Nancy's door and Billy's next call was to John Brannan. He and Annie would be going to Belfast soon and he wanted to make sure there was someone to look out for his daughter and his grand children, should Billy Donnelly come back.

"You wanted to see me, Mr Dawson?" John Brannan stood in front of Billy's desk, his eyes searching for an indication for the summons.

"Sit yourself down John," Billy said, leaning forward, "I need to speak with you about a personal matter and I must ask that it go no further than these four walls.

John Brannan nodded, "understood," he said, "you can trust me."

Billy relaxed, the man had already proved himself trustworthy in the way he'd dealt with Billy Donnelly's attack on Nancy, but now he was going to have to put the weight of protecting his daughter and his grandchildren squarely on the man's shoulders.

"It's about Mrs Donnelly and her family," Billy said, "but Nancy in particular."

John Brannan waited. "As you've already seen, her husband can be a nasty piece of work, especially when the whisky fires him and I won't be around over the next few weeks to look out for her...."

"I understand," John interrupted, quickly, "you can assure your daughter that I'll be willing and able to be of assistance, if she needs it."

Billy smiled, "I know you will," he said, "but it's more than that."

"Nancy and her brood will be moving house very soon to 16 Cowgate...."

Again, John interrupted. "but I live in the Cowgate," he exclaimed in surprise, "three doors up at 22!...."

It was Billy's turn to cut in. "I know," he said, "that's why you're in a perfect position to keep an eye on things for me, but I don't want Nancy to know she's being watched. She thinks she can live quite well on her own, without a man in her life, but you and I know different. This war's turned everything on its head, with women intent on being independent and until things settle down, we men have got to take a step back, but make sure we're there when we're needed."

John nodded sagely. He'd seen the havoc the war had had on both men and women and the 'cease-fire' hadn't returned anything to what it used to be, especially where love and marriage were concerned.

"I see we're 'singing from the same hymn sheet'," Billy said, standing up and extending a hand towards John.  "Let's shake on it then and I'll let you know where you contact me as soon as I can."

"You can count on me, Mr Dawson," John said, returning the handshake and rest assured, I'll keep your daughter and her family safe and sound."

Billy breathed easier as the door closed behind John Brannan. He could do no more for Nancy nor Lexie, for now, his focus would be on Annie and himself and being with their son in Belfast.

John Brannan sang to himself as he returned to the Weaving Flat. He'd already proved himself to be Nancy's protector, now he had the chance to prove he could also be her loving man.

"I'm home," Billy called as he entered the lobby, satisfied that the problems that had begun the day had now been taken care off.

"In here," Annie responded from the kitchen, where Isabella Anderson was sipping tea in silence.

Billy turned questioning eyes on Annie, it wasn't like Isabella to be quiet like this, she was normally full of bounce and energy.

Annie took a deep breath, "money's gone missing from the Hall," she whispered and John Anderson's being accused of taking it."

Billy couldn't believe his ears, "John Anderson a THIEF?" he said, incredulously, "not possible."  When Billy had returned from the fighting in France during the Great War, shell-shocked and barely able to function, it was John Anderson who had saved him from life on the streets as a down-and-out and brought him back to health.

"Isabella," he said gently, "I don't know who's saying these things, but they're not true, not a word of it."

Isabella turned tearful eyes on to Billy.  "I know that," she said, "but the powers that be in the Salvation Army have decided that the best thing would be for John and I to leave the Army and…….."

Annie rushed to her sister-in-law's side, wrapping her arm around her shoulder. "Hush, now Isabella," she said, "God is the only judge and He knows John's not guilty of this charge."

Billy's lips tightened. There it was again, a man's name was about to be blackened and his wife ostracised by the very people she had devoted her life to helping, but as long as God was in his heaven and the churches were filled on Sunday, the godly would rest peacefully in their beds.

Isabella pushed back her chair and stood up as tall as her 5ft 2inches would allow. "I must go," she said, "John needs me more than ever now and I need him."

She hugged Annie. "Be happy, Annie," she said, softly, "and give my love to your wonderful son in Belfast. Tell him he's got the most precious mother and father a boy could wish for."

Annie turned to Billy, after Isabella had left, deep compassion in her heart, now diminished by Isabella's news.

For the rest of the day and evening, Billy's mind was tormented with the thoughts that no matter what he tried to do to keep everyone protected, the 'hand of fate' had a way of letting you know that it, and not you, was in control of everyone's lives and without so much as the touch of a feather, could destroy all the plans mere mortals had for happiness.

———oOo———

# Chapter 25

Billy Donnelly had spent the week sleeping rough and hanging around Chapel doors in search of handouts or some food, to keep him from starvation. He'd considered knocking on Gladys Kelly's door more than once, but he knew he would find it closed and bolted. Gladys may have loved him at one time, but he reasoned that her punishment from God for her life of prostitution would have turned her against him and his Catholic ways forever.

But, before he put his plan into action, he determined to try again to get back into Nancy's good books. The walk to Victoria Road from Lochee took him two hours and by the time he'd reached the close leading to his home, he was almost fainting with hunger and fatigue. He forced himself up the two flights of stairs towards the door, surely, if Nancy had any feelings left in her heart for him at all, she would at least let him in to rest for a while.

But, the door was locked and a look through the kitchen window revealed an empty room. Stunned, Billy banged on a neighbour's door.

"Whit's ah the racket?" came the voice of Annie Henderson, as she opened the door. The sight of the bedraggled Billy Donnelly, his face lost of its handsome looks and his eyes sunken, brought a wave of shock to the woman.

"Where's Nancy," Billy croaked "and the bairns….where's my bairns?"

Annie Henderson felt a wave of compassion for the man, if everything Nancy had told her about him was right, he didn't deserve sympathy, but Annie took him in anyway.

"Here," she said, "drink this." She pushed a cup of tea towards him and a bread roll and watched as he devoured it.

"Nancy's gone," she said as he drained the last of the tea, "and the bairns with her."

Billy felt a wave of panic hit him. "GONE!" he echoed, "GONE WHERE?"

Annie Henderson shrugged her shoulders. "Wha' kens," she said, "a big van turned up twa days ago, loaded up her stuff and that's the last I saw o' her and the bairns."

Billy felt the last of her resolve ebb out of him and he slumped forward onto the table. He'd lost Nancy and his family for good and there was no way back to them.

Annie Henderson sighed. She seen it all before, men going off the rails and expecting their wives to still take them back when it all went wrong and, for Billy Donnelly, it was about as wrong as it was possible to be.

"Look," she said, her pity for the man returning, "ane o' the mill lassies fae doon the stairs says she's gone to live in the Coogate, but that's as much as I ken."

Billy's rheumy eyes blinked and locked onto Annie Henderson's.

"The Cowgate?" he whispered, "are you sure?"

Annie shrugged again. "that's whut I've heard," she said, "tak' it or lave it."

"I'll take it," Billy said, finding energy from somewhere and "you may have just saved my life."

Nancy was singing to herself as she bustled about her new home. Her father had done her proud, the kitchen was spacious and there were two back bedrooms, one for her and Mary Anne and one for wee Billy and Kevin.

She'd be going back to the weaving the next day and thanks to the need for weavers at the Mill during the war, Baxters had opened a nursery for mums to have their bairns minded while they worked. All the horrors of the past were now behind her and the future for them all was taking on a rosy glow.

Billy Donnelly rounded the corner from King Street into the Cowgate, keeping close to the walls and pends as his eyes raked the windows of the tenements for sight of Nancy.  He was shivering from cold and knew he had to get stronger if he was to win his wife back and the only place where he might find a meal and bed for the night was the Salvation Army.  He retraced his steps back up King Street and William Lane to Victoria Road and the Salvation Army Hall.  As usual, the door was open and welcoming and the sound of singing to the brass band filled the air.  Leading the singing was Isabella Anderson.  Billy was in luck. He ducked back into the shadows till the congregation dispersed before inching into the Hall.

"Mrs Anderson," he hissed, "over here."

Isabella turned towards the sound, her eyes squinting into the dimness of the hall porch.

"Show yourself," she said, sternly, "this is a house of God."

Billy stepped into the light. "It's me," he said, "Billy Donnelly."

Isabella beckoned him in, taken aback by his bedraggled frame and thin clothing.

"I'm sorry to bother you," he began, head bowed and fingers locked in front of him, "but I've nowhere else to go and I was hoping the Salvation Army would take me in."

"Does Nancy know you're here?" Isabella asked, hoping he hadn't been threatening her again.

Billy shook his head. "I've no one left," he said, "please…….." Billy legs gave way beneath him and he staggered to a nearby chair, collapsing down into it.

Isabella had seen the disintegration of his marriage to Nancy over the years, but despite his behaviour, she knew too that he'd been a good Catholic boy at the start of it all and was more of a victim than the perpetrator of his wrongdoing.

"The Salvation Army can't help you," she said, firmly, "but I can."

Billy's eyes widened with confusion. "I don't understand," he whimpered, fearing his last hope was being taken out from under him.

"My husband and myself are leaving the Army this very day," she told him "and we won't be coming back." Isabella's voice began to waver, "but our home is open to you till they……..put us out of that."

Billy could hardly believe his ears.

Isabella's eyes levelled with his, "so you see, Billy, you're not the only one who's been turned out of their home."

In the face of Isabella's stoicism, Billy suddenly felt ashamed of himself.  Here he was bemoaning a fate he deserved, while this woman was being dealt the same hand and was facing up to it with courage and selflessness, even opening her door to him, a sinner and outcast, in his hour of need.

Billy stood and saluted Isabella.  "Thank you for the offer" he said, solemnly, "but I won't trouble you any further." Somewhere in Billy's soul, the light of truth had come on and he saw how low he had sunk.

He gazed at the stars, sparkling in the black sky.  "Show me the way," he asked his invisible God, tears filling his eyes "and forgive me, please."

Isabella gathered up her belongings and looked around the empty Hall.  So much of her life had been here and tomorrow... .....well, that was up to God to decide.  She switched off the electric light and closed and locked the door, slipping the key back through the letterbox. She didn't know what the future held for her or her husband, but was certain her faith in God's love would sustain them.  Whether it would sustain Billy Donnelly was another matter but she would pray for him too that night.

It was the week before Christmas and Nancy and her brood were settled in their new home.  The fire blazed in the grate as wee Billy and Mary Anne played Dominos at the kitchen table, while Nancy watched Kevin build a tower of his wooden building blocks only to knock them down again with a delighted giggle.

Everyone stopped their activities, except Kevin, as the sound of knocking at their door brought a tinge of anxiety to the family.

"Do you think it's dad?" wee Billy asked, fear returning to his eyes.

Nancy stood up and walked towards the door, "your dad doesn't know we're here," she whispered, flinching as the knocking was heard again.

"Who's there?" she called out, trying to keep the tremor from her voice.

"John Brannan."

Nancy felt a wave of relief. "It's alright," she said, "it's the man who saved us when your dad broke in."

She opened the door and a cold blast of air blew in along with John Brannan.

"Looks like more snow on the way," he said, smiling at the solemn faces in front of him, as he took off his bonnet and pushed it into his coat pocket.

Nancy was the first to gather her wits together. "I wasn't expecting visitors," she managed to say, wondering how John Brannan knew she was living in the Cowgate now, followed by "is there something wrong?"

John laughed, "just a friendly neighbourly call, to see if there's anything I can do for you," he looked around the kitchen, nodding, "but it looks like you're pretty well sorted."

"Neighbourly?" Nancy queried.

"I've seen you coming and going this past wee while," he said, "I live at number 22, and after what happened at Victoria Road, thought I'd let you know I'm around if…….."

"Thank you, Mr Brannan," Nancy said, interrupting his offer of further help, "but I don't think that'll be necessary," she added, feeling oddly flustered at his presence in her kitchen, "we're all fine."

It wasn't the welcome John had been hoping for, but at least Nancy now knew he was nearby……just in case.

He repositioned the bonnet on his head. "Well, if everything's fine, I'll be going," he said, "just remember I'm close by……"

Nancy closed the door behind him, still feeling unsettled and turned to face her family.

"Cocoa?" she asked, briskly, moving towards the press beside the Main, before anyone could ask any more questions about John Brannan. Something about him was unnerving her, but she couldn't quite put a finger on it.

———oOo———

# Chapter 26

Lexie had well and truly settled into her job as Wing Commander Martin Kettlewell's Private Secretary at RAF Montrose.  As the weeks had gone in, he had taken her more and more into his confidence and trusted her with his Top Secret papers to deal with securely, as well as personal issues relating to his private life.

Apart from when Lexie was at Winnie's home after work, the girls didn't manage to see much of one another, so it was a special treat for both of them to be off duty and spending the day together in Montrose.

"Are you excited about Christmas?" Winnie asked, as they trudged through the snowy streets, stopping every now and then to admire the shop windows with their branches of holly, bunches of mistletoe and strings of coloured decorations.

"I s'ppose," Lexie replied, "but it won't be the same as things were before the war and mum and Billy won't even be in the country!"

Winnie linked her arm through Lexie's.  "You have us you know," she said encouragingly, "dad's ordered a hen from the butcher and mum makes the best 'clootie' dumpling in Scotland."

Lexie smiled and squeezed her friend's hand.  "You're all wonderful," she said "and don't think I don't appreciate all you've done for me, it's just........well, I just feel a bit lonely at times."

Winnie sensed Lexie's sadness and felt lucky to have all the people she loved around her. "C'mon," she said, "let's go to the tearoom by the statue and get warmed up."  Lexie nodded in agreement and followed Winnie across the wide, snow-rutted road. A wave of warmth and the babble of voices met the girls as they went inside, found a cosy seat and ordered tea for two and some shortbread biscuits.

"How many New Year Resolutions are you making this year," Winnie asked, determined to chase Lexie's blues away.

"Haven't thought about it," Lexie replied, sipping the hot tea and feeling its warmth heating her chest.

"Well, think about it!" Winnie insisted, "how about having some fun and letting a handsome airman or two take you out now and then?"

Lexie almost choked on her biscuit.  "I do have fun," she insisted "I just don't have the time for the rest."

Winnie eyed her friend, quizzically, "there's ALWAYS time for 'the rest," she said, wickedly, "if you really put your mind to it."

Lexie put down her cup. "Are you trying to match-make?" she asked, smiling at her friend's efforts to shunt her 'off the shelf' and back into the scary world of relationships.  Lexie had been hurt too often and the thought of putting herself back into 'the fray' was the last thing on her mind.

"I'm only saying…" Winnie continued, "don't give up on love."

Winnie's words hit home.  Had she really given up on loving and being loved? It seemed more like love had given up on her, as her mind sought to understand how she'd ended up alone at Christmas.

That night in bed, Lexie journeyed back in her mind to her first meeting with Robbie, her subsequent rejection of him with her engagement to Charlie Mathieson and how she'd handed back his ring when Robbie had rekindled her love for him.  Then there was Bo, who she'd rejected, again, in favour of marrying Robbie Robertson.  Lexie felt tears begin to flow down her cheeks, for now, Robbie was dead and Lexie was truly alone.

Next morning, Lexie crept out of the house early, not wanting to be reminded of Winnie's words.  She'd have breakfast at the Canteen at the base and just get on with what she was good at, working.

She was clearing a pile of filing when Martin Kettlewell called her into his office.

"Lexie," he said, "I need your help."

"If there's anything I can do," she said, "please ask."

Martin cleared his throat. "Well," he said, "it's a bit of an imposition and you don't have to agree, what with it being Christmas and all......"

"It's alright," Lexie interrupted him, "I haven't any plans for Christmas, so I'd be pleased to be of service."

Martin Kettlewell relaxed. He had to get this next bit right, for his nephew's sake.

"It's just this, Lexie," he said, leaning forward in his chair, "my nephew and his son are coming to stay with me over Christmas and, hopefully, into the New Year...."

"Yes?" Lexie queried, wondering where this was going.

"Well," Martin continued, "the Base is holding a Christmas Party for the children of the personnel and I was wondering if you could perhaps.....take charge of little Louie at the party?"

Lexied blinked. Looking after a little boy at the Christmas Party, seemed like a strange request, but Winnie's words returned to her mind. 'Don't give up on love' she'd said and here was a little boy, also alone in a strange new world, like her.

"Of course I can look after him," she said, firmly, "Louie, is it?"

Martin Kettlewell relaxed, he'd done his bit by bringing Lexie and Louie together, the rest was out of his hands.

The Wing Commanded beamed. "The party is on Saturday and I'll bring Louie here to meet you before it starts."

Lexie nodded her agreement. "I'll be here," she said, "around 1'oclock?"

"1 o'clock will be perfect," Martin said, kindly, "and thank you Lexie," he added "for everything."

Lexie was a bit perplexed at the words, but put it down to the Christmas spirit. "My pleasure," she said, making her way back to her connecting office. Lexie had no experience of children, except the occasional visit to Nancy and her bairns, especially warming to King Kevin, who'd stolen her heart the minute she'd seem him.

"Louie," she muttered, "what a strange name for a boy."

Annie and Billy were packed and would be leaving Dundee behind today and heading off on their trip to Belfast. Billy had written to their son, John Adams, who would meet them at the dock where their ship was to berth.

One of Billy's workers would be driving them to the Railway Station and making sure their motor was safely garaged and looked after till their return, whenever that would be.

Annie was busying herself with checking windows and doors and boiling the kettle for their final cup of tea before departure. She had ticked off everything on her 'to do' list, satisfied that everyone who needed to know, now knew of their impending journey. It had all helped to keep her nerves at bay, but now it was nearly time to go, she started worrying about how Lexie would be all alone at Christmas, whether Billy Donnelly would turn up at Nancy's again and threaten her, how Isabella and John Anderson would manage without the Salvation Army and Billy could see the lines of worry forming on her brow. And what about Ian, she fretted, her son with her late husband, Euan McPherson? Was the letter she'd sent him enough to reassure him that she loved him too and that although they now lived miles apart, she was still his mother.

"Everything will be alright," she heard Billy say as he poured her some tea.

Annie's eyes met his. He was only man she'd really loved and now, at last, they were together and going to be with their son in Belfast.

She felt a wave of love for Billy, who'd never stopped loving her, even when she'd married Alex Melville and then Euan, determined she'd live without him in her life. So much water had flowed under the bridge since that fateful coupling so many years ago and now, the circle was complete and what should have happened then, was happening now.

"Do we deserve this happiness?" she asked, methodically tidying away the teapot and cups." Billy smiled at his wife, turning her round to face him, "no one deserves it more," he told her, kissing the tear from her eye, "so ease your mind, Annie Pepper, the rest of our life is waiting."

The loud knocking on the door broke into the moment of love. "That'll be Tam and he'll have the motor running," Billy said, "so get your coat on and we'll be off." Annie took one last look round.  "Yes, Billy," she said," her heart overflowing with love for him.  "I'm ready."

# Chapter 27

Billy Donnelly slept in an empty concrete air raid shelter that night, with only his thoughts for company. He knew for sure that Nancy had loved him once. He'd made her pregnant, despite his fear of the priests and Joe Cassiday, but had to be forced by her father, Billy Dawson, to marry her. Was that where it had all gone wrong, he wondered?

Then, when wee Billy had been born, the doctor's warning had seeped into his very soul, "if you get your wife pregnant again, Mr Donnelly, it could kill her." He felt a surge of anger at the words that had made him afraid to love Nancy again and fear of the priests if he'd tried to prevent another pregnancy.

Images of Gladys Kelly filled his head. The prostitute had been his only option, he reasoned, his lust couldn't be controlled and he'd gone back to her again and again for relief. Didn't Billy Dawson understand that!

Billy Dawson, Nancy's father and Billy's nemesis, reared up in his mind. If only he'd kept out of things, he and Nancy would still be together.

Billy could feel hot anger coursing through his veins. If only he wasn't around, Nancy would believe him again and take him back.

A rat scuttled past him in the darkness and he struck a match, lighting up the stark walls of the shelter. Yes, he decided, his brain feverish with hunger and isolation. Billy Dawson had to die and he knew how to kill him.

By the time he'd walked through the snow to King Street and Baxters Mill, Billy was ravenous. Most shops were still shuttered, but Harry Duncan's butcher shop was lit from inside. Billy stopped at the window gazing at the pies on display, the smell of a further batch cooking in the back shop, reaching his nostrils and emphasising his hunger, all thoughts of reeking revenge on Billy Dawson temporarily forgotten.

If he could just get that door open, he reasoned, he could reach in and grab one or two. Leaning his weight against the wooden frame, he pushed against it, but the door remained firmly closed. He'd have to force his way in.

Taking a step back, he was about to shoulder the door open, when a large hand gripped the collar of his jacket. "Not intending to break in now, are you?" a deep Irish voice asked.

Billy froze. The other hand of Police Sergeant Murchison clamped a handcuff on his wrist and quickly brought the other wrist behind Billy's back  to meet the same fate.  However, on turning him round to face him, recognition suddenly dawned in the Sergeant's eyes. He looked closer....."Donnelly?" he queried, "Billy Donnelly?"

Billy nodded. Sergeant Murchison had been a Police Constable when Sergeant MacPherson had been in charge at Bell Street Station and he'd been tasked with watching the 'comings and goings' of Nancy Donnelly, especially on Saturday nights at the Palais de Dance.

Billy Donnelly was a Scots Guard then, fighting Hitler and Sergeant Murchison had had to report back that Billy's wife was indeed 'entertaining a man' while her husband was away at war.

"What's happened to you man?" he asked, shocked at Billy's gaunt appearance.  "A Scots Guard looking to rob a butcher's shop!"

Billy hung his head and tears of despair began to drip off the end of his frozen nose.

Sergeant Murchison took out his keys and unlocked the handcuffs.

"C'mon," he said, "it's hot food and a warm coat you need and I know just the place."

Sergeant Murchison telephoned Bell Street from the nearby blue Police Box and ordered a Police Van to be sent to King Street. Billy Donnelly looked so weak, the sergeant was concerned he'd collapse in the street if he made Billy walk.

"Where are we going?" Billy asked, once he'd been bundled into the back of the Black Maria, visions of being shut in a police cell forming in his mind.  He'd visited his father at Bell Street years since, when he'd been accused of fraud and the iron grimness and smells of that place had never left him.

"I told you," Sergeant Murchison said, "to get you a hot meal and warm clothing then you and me are going to have a wee talk," he added, "just the two of us."

The Salvation Army had opened a shelter for the homeless in a building across from the jail and frequently took vagrant men into their care, often saving their lives, when all else had turned against them.

Sergeant Murchison spoke briefly to the smiling face under the Salvation Army bonnet, nodding towards Billy before leaving.

Billy was beyond emotion as he looked around the room where he'd been taken and in the dimness he could see mattresses, wall to wall, some supporting ragged bodies under the thin blankets.  The noises of whimpering and snoring men filled his ears, their suffering far worse than Billy's had ever been. Slowly, his self pity and resentment began to ebb, replaced by shame and remorse for all he'd put Nancy and his bairns through. No wonder she'd kicked him out, he deserved all he'd got.

The smiling Salvationist came back into the room.

"C'mon, Mr Donnelly," she said, kindly, "there's hot soup and bread in the canteen and we've found an Army greatcoat for you that'll keep the frost out."

Billy stood and followed the young girl.  The heat in the canteen wafted over him and the hot soup and bread brought life back to his frozen limbs. The Army coat was placed on a chair beside him and a mug of hot tea and plate of jam sandwiches was placed in front of him.

Silently, Billy ate the food and thanked God for the Salvation Army, without them, he wouldn't have survived another night on the streets and he determined, more than ever, that he would make it up to Nancy and never commit another sin as long as he lived.

It was late in the afternoon before Sergeant Murchison returned to the hostel. "How's he been?" he asked the Officer in charge. "Better than he was when you brought him in," she said, "but we can't keep him here forever," she added "and he's not in real need like the others here, so he can stay the night, but after that....?"

Sergeant Murchison didn't know quite what to do about Billy Donnelly, only that something had to be done, or the man would end up either in jail or dead.

"Mr Donnelly," he said, pulling up a chair next to Billy in the Canteen, "I see you've been fed and that warm coat," he nodded towards the Army Greatcoat, "will keep out any weather Scotland has to offer."

Billy forced a weak smile.

"The Sallies tell me you can bide the night here," the sergeant said, "but that's all and as I don't want to have to catch you robbing shops again,

tell me, Billy, where do you go from here?"

Billy met his eyes. "Nowhere," he said, flatly, "I've nowhere to go and nobody to go to."

"What about that wife of yours" the Sergeant asked? his brow furrowing with concern, "or your family for that matter."

"Gone," he was told, "all gone."

In a voice devoid of emotion, Billy told the policeman the whole sorry saga, missing out nothing and expecting nothing back. The sergeant had helped him once, which was more than he deserved and he expected nothing more, but Sergeant Murchison had one more trick up his sleeve.

He patted Billy on the shoulder. "Sleep here tonight," he said, "I'll be back the morn' with someone you need to meet."

Billy blinked in confusion, "who?" he asked, for a split second hoping the sergeant meant Nancy.

"You'll see," came the answer, "just get some sleep and I'll be back in the mornin'."

Billy caught his sleeve, "why are you helping me?" he asked, unable to understand kindness, "no one's ever helped me before, except for Gladys Kelly."

The sergeant released Billy's grip. "I'm no Gladys Kelly," he said, smiling, "but I'm an Irish Catholic too and I know the fear the priests wield over us. But I also know that underneath, you're a good man Billy Donnelly."

Nancy was at her looms, working the jute into hessian cloth and looking forward to Christmas with her sons and daughter when the shuttle jammed and the loom had to be shut down.

She signalled for a Tenter to deal with the problem, but along with him came John Brannan.

"Having a bit of bother?" he shouted above the noise.

Nancy indicated the Tenter beside him. "Not for much longer," she said, stating the obvious.

But John Brannan signalled for her to follow him to the exit door from the Weaving Flat.

Confused, she followed him away from the noise and into the quietness of the corridor.

"Is there something wrong?" Nancy asked, anxiously, hoping that King Kevin hadn't upset any of the other bairns at the Nursery and would have to be taken home.

"Nothing's wrong," John said, smiling at her, "I was just wondering," he continued, looking out of the frosted window, "about Christmas."

Nancy frowned. "Christmas!" she exclaimed, "what about Christmas?"

John cleared his throat, "well, I was wondering if I could maybe share the day with you and your family.....or just part of it," he hastened to add, quickly realising Nancy hadn't given him a thought."

Nancy's frown deepened. She knew she was thankful to the man for rescuing her from Billy's assault, but did he think her gratitude extended to something more......?

Nancy was no fool when it came to men, but her fingers had been badly burned when she'd reached out to Jim Murphy for love when Billy had been away fighting the Germans, but the misery that had brought her remained buried deep in her heart and was now surfacing again at John Brannan's suggestion.

But before she could come up with an answer, the dinner-time bummer sounded and the heavy rubber doors leading to the weaving flat burst open, disgorging the workers into the corridor.

"Sorry," she mouthed, over her shoulder as she joined the rush to the canteen, leaving John Brannan behind and his question unanswered.

# Chapter 28

Lexie presented herself at the Wing Commander's Office on Christmas Eve morning to meet Louie and try to keep him amused until the party that afternoon. Her stomach was a little knotted at the prospect of 'mothering' the little boy, but she reminded herself that she'd minded King Kevin in the past and, although Louie was a bit older, she was sure she'd cope.

Lexie knocked and entered Martin Kettlewell's office, where Martin was saluting a very small Wing Commander, who Lexie could just see peeping out from under Martin's RAF hat.

"Ah!" he said, "Lexie, come in, come in. Meet our new Wing Commander of the Day, Louie Lafayette."

Lexie couldn't suppress a grin as the biggest pair of dark brown eyes emerged from under the now tipped up hat.

Lexie stood to attention and saluted briskly. "Reporting for duty Sir," she said, "at your service."

Louie giggled, "Bon jour, Madam," he said, "merci."

"You're speaking French!" Lexie exclaimed, before realising that the child's name should have made that obvious.

"His mother was French," Martin said, quietly, "he's bilingual, so don't let him fool you into thinking he doesn't understand what you're saying, it's more he wants to get out of doing something, like eating all his vegetables, isn't that right Louie?"

The child handed Martin his hat and Lexie saw his full face for the first time. Dark hair ruffled over his forehead and a wide grin spread across his face at the sight of Lexie's surprised look.

What a handsome young boy, Lexie thought and so tall for his age. "He's tall for his age," Lexie said aloud, "and very handsome too," she added, warming to the brown-eyed boy.

"He takes his looks from his father," Martin said, hoping Lexie might somehow make a connection. "My nephew's a Wing Commander like myself, but he can't be with us this morning as he has a very pressing engagement later that can't be broken."

Lexie thought she saw a glimpse of mischief in the Winco's eyes, but just nodded acceptance of the explanation..

"The Christmas Party isn't 'till 1 o'clock," Martin said, "so, why don't you show Louie around and let him see the aircraft we have here and maybe even let him sit in the cockpit of a Spitfire!" He turned to Louie who was wide-eyed at the chance, "would you like that?"

"Yes please," Louie said, reverting to English, "can we go now?" he asked, turning to Lexie.

"Of course," Lexie smiled, "and we can have hot cocoa and biscuits at the Canteen."

"Lexie means cookies," Martin said, seeing Louie's confused face, "and hot chocolate."

It was Lexie's turn to look confused. "It's what Canadians call it," he added, watching as the word reached Lexie's consciousness.

"Canadian," she whispered to herself. "Louie's Canadian?" she asked, looking again at the dark haired child, but before she could say anymore, Martin ushered the pair out of his office.

"Have fun," he called after them and see you both at the Party."

Martin returned to his desk and breathed a sigh of relief, he'd done as Bo had asked and put Lexie and Louie together, the rest would be up to his nephew.

Louie's excitement at seeing the various aircraft was infectious and Lexie began to enjoy showing him around the base and introducing him to the Ground Crew who were making sure the aircraft were ready for the pilots. Question after question was thrown at Lexie, as Louie wanted to know how everything worked.

"He's a clever one," a crewman said, delighted to explain as much as possible to Louie about the Spitfire "and I think the Wing Commander has said you could sit in the cockpit....if you like," he said, winking at Lexie.

"Just like his dad," the man added, "can't get enough of flying."

Lexie's ears pricked up. "His dad?" she asked, "do you know him?"

"Sure do," he replied, reaching up to lift Louie into the Spitfire.

"But it's a secret who he is," the crewman said, making the motion of a zip closing across his lips, "but Louie's going to see him later today," he added, "so 'keep mum' till then."

Lexie was getting more confused than ever. "A secret?" she repeated, but the crewman had gone, whistling to himself as he went.

At the Canteen, the cookies and hot chocolate were scoffed by Lexie and Louie and, right on time, the snow began to fall again, covering everything in a blanket of white.

"I hope Santa can find his way here through all this snow," Lexie said, finishing her cocoa and feeling its warmth spreading through to the tips of her chilly fingers.

"Santa likes the snow," her young companion advised her, "at home, it's lots more than this and he always manages to get through."

"Home?" Lexie queried, trying to rid her head of the confusion that was forming about the boy, "where's home then, Louie?"

"Oh, you wouldn't know it," Louie said, in a matter of fact voice, munching on another biscuit. "It's called Quebec."

Lexie frowned, she'd heard the name but had no idea where in Canada it was and before she could ask any more questions, Louie changed the subject.

"Do you have any children?" Louie asked, sounding older than his years.

"No," Lexie said, "no I don't", taken aback by the blunt question.

"Papa's great," he said, looking into the middle distance, but I'd like a brother to play with."

Lexie felt a tear of concern for the child and chided herself for the self-pity she had indulged in when Annie and Billy had announced their plan to spend Christmas in Belfast with their son, John Adams.

And now, here was this child before her, facing being alone, except for his father and, like Lexie, with no other family to share Christmas with.

She glanced at her wristwatch. "C'mon," she said, forcing the smile back on her face, "time for you and me to go to the Party, we don't want to miss all the fun."

The snow was getting heavier and it was with some relief that they got to the Drill Hall where the party was being held. The Base personnel had done a great job of decorating the hall with brightly coloured paper chains, balloons and tinsel and a huge Christmas tree twinkled in a corner with painted baubles, tiny lights and a glittering star on top.

Long tables had been set with all manner of goodies to eat, mostly baked by the Canteen, but the women at the Base had managed to produce a large Christmas cake using up the Food Ration Coupons of everyone who could spare them.

Children and their mums and dads were arriving almost simultaneously, but Louie clung to Lexie's hand, watching as the number of youngsters increased and the noise and excitement heightened.

No wonder Louie was overwhelmed, but Lexie knew she had to get him to mix with the others, or he'd end up miserable.

"C'mon," she said, leading him to one of the tables, "let's see what's for eating."

Lexie spotted an empty seat beside a little girl, who also seemed a bit lost and ushered Louie to sit next to her. "This is Louie," she said to the girl, kneeling down between them, he's from a place called Canada.

A sweet face framed by blonde curls and set with big blue eyes, looked into Louie's brown ones. "My name's Janet," she said shyly "and my dad fixes the Spitfires." Lexie breathed a sigh of relief. That was the best thing Janet could have said and she grinned as Louie's eyes lit up. "Really," he said, all worries evaporating, "I've been in the cockpit of a Spitfire!" he announced proudly.

Lexie stood up, and stepped back as the two heads nodded and began chattering to one another. Louie would be fine, she thought, he may not have found a brother, but Janet and her Spitfire dad would do just fine instead.

Out of the corner of her eye Lexie could see someone waving furiously.

Winnie was weaving her way through the mayhem towards her.

"Isn't it great?" she said, breathlessly. "Our first Christmas without fear of being bombed or invaded by Hitler and the bairns are in for a big surprise."

Again, Lexie seemed to be the only one who wasn't in on the secret.

"What surprise," she asked. Winnie eyes widened in amazement, "don't you know who's coming?" she asked.

"No," Lexie said, "who's coming?"

"SANTA CLAUSE, of course," Winnie mouthed theatrically, ssshhhing Lexie from asking anything further. "But the bairns don't know," she said, glancing over her shoulder in case a little one was near enough to hear "and he's got a present for every one of them."

"Well, as long as he has one for little Louie," Lexie said, pointing to her charge, "he's come a long way to be here."

Winnie looked over at the child. "Who's Louie?"

Lexie pulled her clear of the melee. He's the son of "Wing Commander Kettlewell's nephew and he's asked me to look after him till his dad gets here."

Winnie shrugged at the news before getting back to her excitement at seeing Santa Clause. "Can you hear bells jingling?" Winnie suddenly queried, straining her ears. Lexie listened, beginning to catch on to Winnie's excitement at Santa's arrival. "I think I can," she said, "yes, they're getting louder."

A hush was descending on the Hall as one by one, the children also heard the jingling bells and a whisper ran round the room.

"Santa's here!"

All eyes turned towards the big Hall doors as they swung open and there, sitting in a real sleigh pulled by a real deer, was Santa Clause. His red coat and trousers were topped with a fur trimmed hat, as he stepped down from the sleigh and swinging a huge sack over his shoulder, Santa Clause came in from the cold.

The whole place suddenly erupted in cheering and clapping as Santa made his way toward the Christmas tree and set his sack down. Beaming around at all the bairns and calling out "Merry Christmas everyone," he waved and grinned, beckoning to the mums to bring their little ones to him to get their present.

Louie had latched onto Lexie again, his eyes wide with wonder at the red clad figure with the big white beard. "Do you want me to come with you," Lexie whispered, "when it's your turn?"

Louie nodded, but remained waiting till he was the last one left to get his present.

While all the others opened their parcels and showed one another their gifts, Santa beckoned Louie over.

"It's your turn," Lexie said, keeping hold of his hand as they approached.

When he was close enough, Santa whispered something in his ear.

Amazed, Louie threw his arms around him. "Papa!" he exclaimed, "it's me, Louie."

Lexie caught her breath. Santa Clause was Louie's father? So, that was the secret everyone was keeping! She felt tears of emotion fill her eyes, Louie and his papa would be together for Christmas after all.

Martin Kettlewell seemed to appear out of nowhere, Lexie suddenly finding him standing next to her. "One happy boy," he said, nodding towards Louie, "and one happy Papa," Lexie replied, her eyes still misty with tears.

"I think Santa will want to thank you for looking after Louie till he got here," Martin said, quietly, "he'll be bringing Louie to my quarters once everyone leaves, so maybe you could come there in an hour say."

Lexie nodded, watching as Louie and his father were escorted through a side door. "Of course," she said, "I'll just help with the tidying up first."

"Understood," Martin said, sensing Lexie's need to be alone for a while.

But Lexie wasn't alone for long, Winnie came rushing over.

"Wasn't that just great?" she said, "the bairns loved seeing Santa."

Lexie felt a wave of self-pity sweep over her again, "Louie had his dad, Winnie had her family, Annie and Billy had John Adams and Ian had his new wife in Carlyle, but she had no one.

"Is everything alright?" she heard Winnie say, seeing the change of mood coming over Lexie. "What's wrong?"

Lexie swallowed hard. "Nothing's wrong," she said, forcing a smile, "now let's help get things cleared up here," she murmured, "tomorrow's Christmas Day and everyone will want time to be with their families."

After an hour of brisk activity, Lexie felt calmer. It's just another day, she told herself, as she headed towards the Wing Commander's quarters, then everything would be back to normal.

Her knock was answered by Louie, rushing to greet her. "Papa was helping Santa Clause give out presents," he told Lexie, "real Santa's stuck in the snow in Moose Jaw."

Lexie stood perfectly still. "Moose Jaw!" she exclaimed, "but you live in Quebec...... don't you?"

Louie shook his head, "that's just where I was born," he said, with childlike patience, "me and Papa live in Moose Jaw."

"You remember Moose Jaw don't you Lexie?"

Lexie turned towards the owner of the deep Canadian voice. "BO?"

"The same," Bo said, "and I hope you're pleased to see me."

Lexie felt she was going to faint, as a rush of emotion hit her. Bo McGhee, the man she'd turned down in order to marry Robbie, was standing in front of her, his Santa Clause suit replaced by the uniform of a Wing Commander of the Royal Canadian Air Force.

"I think Lexie needs a drink," Bo said to his Uncle, as he guided Lexie to a chair and maybe Louie could have some lemonade in the kitchen.

Martin nodded, taking the hint. "Sure, Bo," he said, "there's whisky and soda on the sideboard," he told him, as he ushered Louie out of the door.

"I didn't mean to shock you," he said, handing Lexie her drink, "but I had to see you again, once I knew you were here at Montrose."

Lexie's voice had completely deserted her, as it always had when faced with overwhelming emotion. Memories of meeting Bo at Lossiemouth, falling in love with him and boarding the ship to Halifax to marry him and live in Canada filled her head. But, she'd married Robbie and must have hurt Bo unbearably, yet, here he was and wanting to see her again!

She could see he was looking for an answer to confirm she still felt something, anything, for him, but Lexie could only shake and stare, as though she'd seen a ghost.

Bo's lips tightened. It had been a mistake, too much water had flowed under the bridge and Lexie had moved on and felt nothing for him.

"I'm sorry," he said, "I had hoped....." he hung his head, "but I see I've just upset you."

Before Lexie could respond, he left the room and returned with Louie and Martin Kettlewell.

"Louie has something to say to you," he said, nodding to his son to speak.

The child stepped forward and took hold of Lexie's hand. "I thank you very much," he said, "for being my friend."

Lexie blinked away a tear, her heart breaking at the small, solemn face in front of her.

"Maybe we'll meet again," she said, "or you could write me a letter from Moose Jaw." Louie turned to his father. "May I, Papa?"

Bo smiled, "Of course you may," he said, "and if Lexie wishes, she can join us for Christmas Day, before we fly back home. That's unless you've got a family celebration to go to?" he added, hoping she hadn't.

Lexie stood on wobbly legs. "I'll think about it," she said, almost in a whisper. "Goodnight Louie," she said "and thank you for being my friend too."

The snow went unnoticed as Lexie made her way back to Winnie's house, her mind and emotions conflicted by the sight of Bo again.

She quickly went through to her room, almost ignoring the welcoming voices of Winnie and her parents, she had to calm down and let her inner feelings about what had just happened, come to the surface.

Had she let the time of year heighten her emotions, was it the child, Louie, who had touched her heart, or was there still something deep inside that could be rekindled? Lexie slept badly that night, but by morning she knew what she had to do.

# Chapter 29

Billy was wakened from a fractured sleep by the arrival of Sergeant Murchison. "Get yourself presentable?" he told Billy, "we'll be in the Canteen."

"Right," Billy replied, struggling to his feet and running his fingers through his tousled hair. After trying a few doors, he found himself in a dimly lit lavatory with a sink set under the frosted window. He looked at himself in the cracked mirror balanced on the window ledge. His face was sprouting a rough and shaggy beard and his teeth were yellow, even when he'd been fighting in France, he'd never looked as wretched as he did now.

"Get yourself presentable!" he murmured in disbelief, unsure if he'd ever be presentable again,as he splashed the ice cold water over his face, scooping a handful into his mouth to try to wash out the debris of sleep.

He found a piece of broken comb discarded on a shelf and tried, unsuccessfully, to tame his hair.

The Canteen was quiet, but the women were busy preparing food for their charges when Billy entered.

"Over here," the sergeant waved. Warily, Billy sat down, conscious that the policeman was not alone, beside him sat another sergeant, but this one was dressed in the uniform of the Scots Guards.

"Meet my brother," Sergeant Murchison said. Instinctively, Billy stood up and saluted. The soldier smiled, "old habits die hard I see," as he returned the salute.

"Michael has a proposition for you," the policeman said, "which just might save your sorry life."

Billy sat very still. All he wanted was to get back with Nancy and had hoped Sergeant Murchison was going to suggest intervening on his behalf but, plainly, this wasn't going to happen.

Michael Murchison leant forward over the table. "Mr Donnelly," he said, "my brother tells me you're considering turning to crime to keep yourself fed." Billy nodded, a tinge of shame returning to his soul as he remembered Harry Duncan's butcher shop and the pies.

"He's also told me that you're a good Catholic boy, like us and thinks that you deserve a second chance." Billy's brain began to focus on the words. "Second chance," he echoed, "I don't want a second chance," he said, "I just want my wife back."

The brothers glanced at one another. "The state you're in Mr Donnelly," Michael intoned, "she won't give you a second glance, never mind a second chance."

Billy felt his temper bristle as he stood up, "thanks to both of you," he said, "but I'll take care of my own business and that includes my wife."

Michael Murchison nodded in acceptance. "I've seen your Army Records Billy," he said, "you were a good man and fought bravely," he extended his hand to shake Billy's, "if you change your mind," he said, "just let me know," but no answer came from Billy's tight lips.

Both Sergeant Murchisons' shrugged at the negative response. They'd done their best to get Billy back on the straight and narrow, but he wasn't having any of it.

"I wish you luck then," said the policeman, "but next time I catch you thieving," he added ominously, "it'll be the jail for you."

Billy ate the hot porridge and bread roll and tea, before pulling on the Army Greatcoat. He turned the collar up and thrust his hands in the pockets, he had to find Nancy, make her understand and get her to take him back.

Nancy finished her shift, avoiding eye contact with John Brannan and hurrying out of the Weaving Flat before he had a chance to speak to her again about Christmas Day. That evening, she planned to clean the house from top to bottom with the help of Mary Anne and wee Billy and she'd managed to save enough money to buy one of Harry Duncan's chicken's for their Christmas Dinner, which was wrapped and waiting in the larder.

"What's the hurry," she heard a male voice say, as she turned into the Cowgate and home.  Nancy froze as a hand gripped her shoulder.  Billy's voice was unmistakable and she felt a wave of panic seize her.  Had she not recognized his voice, she wouldn't have known the shabby figure before her, as she turned to face her husband.

"What do you want?" she asked, trying to keep the tremor out of her voice while releasing her arm.  She was outside in the street, people were around, she reasoned, he wouldn't dare try anything to hurt her in full view of witnesses.

"I just want to speak with you," Billy said, "but not here, take me home with you," he begged, "I promise I won't do anything to hurt you again."

Nancy took a step away, "I've nothing to say to you Billy," she said, "just go away and leave us alone."

"WAIT," he said, desperation beginning to turn to anger at Nancy's refusal to listen to him, "you don't realise....I've changed, I'm not the man I used to be, just give me a chance!"

People were beginning to glance across at them, wondering what was going on and Nancy was aware that Mary Anne would be bringing Kevin home from the nursery in an hour and she wanted Billy gone by then.

"Alright," she finally agreed, "but when I ask you to go, you'll go!"

Billy relaxed, once he was back in, he'd be going nowhere.


Full of misgivings, Nancy opened the door and let her husband in.

Billy looked around the large kitchen.  "This is better than Victoria Road," he said, huffily, "I suppose your dad had something to do with it?"

At once, Nancy realised she'd made a mistake.  Nothing had changed, Billy still hated her father and she'd been a fool to let him anywhere near her.

"What is it you wanted to say?" Nancy asked, keeping her back to the unlocked door in case she had to make a run for it.

"Nancy, Nancy," Billy whined, "what's so wrong about wanting to be with my wife, the woman I love."

Nancy almost laughed. "LOVE," she echoed, "like you loved me when you were bedding Gladys Kelly."

Nancy had hit a nerve. "Is that what this is all about?" he shouted, anger seeping back into his heart, "and what about Jim bloody Murphy," he countered, "how do you think that felt, fighting for King and country only to find my wife had been entertaining her fancy man in MY BED."

Nancy's blood ran cold, as before, Billy was getting out of control and she knew she had to get out of there.

Turning quickly, she ran for the door with Billy in pursuit. "WAIT!" he shouted, "COME BACK," but Nancy was out the door and running, straight into the arms of John Brannan.

She swung behind him, pushing him forward to face Billy as he came careering through the door after her.

For a split second, no one reacted, then John Brannan's voice could be heard, calm and determined.

"I think your wife wants you to go Mr Donnelly," he said, inching Nancy further away from the two of them.

"Do you now," Billy said, menacingly, "make way for you to come in, I suppose!" The words hung in the air between them. "Well, it'll be over my dead body," Billy spat, taking a step closer to John, "if your man enough, that is?"

"STOP IT! STOP IT!" Nancy screamed. "Just go Billy, please!"

But Billy wasn't for going and neither was John Brannan.

"I'd better warn you," Billy sneered, loosening the Army overcoat, "I was in the Scots Guards during the war and I'd be pleased to add another dead man to my tally."

"Do your worst," John said, "but one way or another, you'll be leaving Nancy alone from now on, just like Billy Dawson wants."

Billy flinched, where was Billy Dawson in all this, was the man going to ruin his life forever? But the mention of his father-in-law's name seemed to stop him in his tracks and he pushed past John Brannan and Nancy, cursing as he went. "SLUT," he hissed, at her "once a slut always a slut."

John listened till the sound of Billy's footsteps faded away, before turning his attention back to Nancy, who was shaking with cold and fear.

"Come inside, Nancy," he said, taking her arm, "everything's going to be alright."

By the time Mary Anne arrived with Kevin, Nancy had stopped shaking and John Brannan had left, assuring her that he'd be keeping an eye open for the rest of Christmas Eve "just in case," as he'd put it.

But, he knew a bully when he saw one and Billy Donnelly fitted the bill. He'd met men like him when he too had served in the Scots Guards during the war, full of bravado when facing the weak, but cowering in the face of strength.

The snow had stopped and the Cowgate was eerily quiet, as the street lights came on and Dundee folk drew their curtains and locked their doors.  Only the bairns wanted to watch at the window till Santa Clause came by but by the time 8 o'clock chimed, they were all fast asleep.

But John Brannan was awake and stayed that way till gone midnight....just incase.

# Chapter 30

Christmas Day dawned, clear and cold.  The snow had stopped, leaving everything glistening under the moonlight.  Lexie switched on the little bedside lamp and squinted at the hands of her watch. 5.30 am.

She flopped back onto her pillow and allowed her thoughts to surface, reliving the moment when she'd turned and Bo had been standing there, his tall frame seeming to fill the room, as everything else had faded into the background.  Had this really happened?  Since her decision to marry Robbie, she had forced Bo out of her mind along with the hurt she'd seen in his eyes when she'd returned his ring at the dockside in Halifax.  And yet, here he was, back in her life once more.........?

Slowly, she got up and slipping on her dressing gown, tiptoed to the kitchen.  Filling the kettle, she set in on the stove to boil and pulled back the curtains.  The sky was ablaze with stars and a full moon was setting in the West. Lexie looked in awe at the scene, smiling to herself as an image of Santa Clause and his sleigh skimming through the snow towards her filled her mind. The hiss of steam from the boiling kettle broke through the reverie and Lexie hurried to switch off the gas ring, before it started whistling.

"You're up early," she heard the sleepy voice of Bertha Adams say, "I'm usually the first, but if you're making a pot of tea, I wouldn't say no."

"Mrs Adams!" Lexie exclaimed, caught by surprise at her landlady's entry, "I didn't mean to wake anyone, I'm sorry....." Bertha shook her head, "no need to apologise Lexie," she smiled, "in Summer I'm up earlier than this.  Now, where's that tea?"

Lexie quickly filled the teapot with the boiling water and brought it to the table.  Bertha had already set out the cups and the two early birds sat facing one another, quietly, sipping the brew.

"Looking for Santa Clause then were you?" Bertha quipped, smiling and nodding towards the  window.  "Sort of," Lexie replied, softly, wondering if Bertha Adams could have read her thoughts.

Bertha leant forward and touched Lexie's hand.  "You don't still believe in Santa Clause do you?" she asked, gently, sensing something was wrong.  Lexie felt her chin begin to quiver, Bertha was right, there was no such person as Santa Clause, whether  Bo McGhee came disguised as him or not.

"I don't know what to do," Lexie murmured, simply.

Bertha looked at the sadness in the young girl's eyes.

"Don't know what to do about what, Lexie?" she asked.

Lexie felt her throat tighten and couldn't speak.

"If you don't tell me what's wrong, lassie," Berth urged, "then I can't help you."


Bertha waited, till eventually, in the quietness of Christmas morning, Lexie began to speak of the past, of her love for Robbie and her rejection of Bo McGhee, when she chose marriage to Robbie instead of him, leaving Bo broken hearted.

"And now," Lexie whispered, "Bo is here, at the Base, with his son....." her eyes met Bertha's "and I don't know what to do?"

The older woman leant back in her chair.  "Will he be at the Base for long?" she asked, "give you a little time to see how you feel about him again?"

Lexie shook her head, "They fly back to Canada tomorrow," she said, taking a deep breath and voicing Bo's invitation.  "I'm invited for Christmas Dinner with Bo and Louie today, but........I don't know if I should go and maybe end up ruining everyone's Christmas."

Bertha Adams nodded.  "It sounds like it's all been a bit of a shock, Lexie and I'm sure this Bo doesn't expect you to fly into his arms after all that's gone on in the past."

Lexie blinked away the threatening tears. Bertha was right, no one expected her to do anything other than join Bo and his son for Christmas Dinner and it would be good to spend time with them before they went back to Moose Jaw, Lexie reasoned and with no family of her own to visit........

"You're right," she said, firmly, "and little Louie is adorable..."she added, pushing back her chair and standing up. "Thanks Mrs Adams," she said, "I think I've just been a bit overwhelmed with the surprise of seeing Bo again, but I feel better now we've spoken and I will go for Christmas Dinner and enjoy it."

The kitchen door flew open and Winnie rushed in. "Merry Christmas everyone," she squealed, "isn't it just wonderful, with the snow and Santa Clause at the Base and........" Winnie suddenly became aware of the lack of enthusiasm from her mother and Lexie. "Is something wrong?" she asked. Bertha quickly realised that Winnie knew nothing about Bo McGhee and Lexie's dilemma and deftly changed the subject.

"The only thing wrong is you carrying on like a wee bairn," she said, grinning at her daughter, "now away and make yourself decent and then help me with the breakfast or there'll be no present for you from Santa!"

Winnie threw up her hands in mock-horror, "NO PRESENT FROM SANTA!" she said, hurrying out of the door, "best get going then. See you at breakfast Lexie."

Bertha hugged Lexie. "Merry Christmas, lassie," she said, "now go and make yourself pretty and don't you worry about a thing, if this Bo McGhee is half the man you think he is, then he'll do what's right by you."

At noon, Lexie pulled on her snow boots and fastened her coat up to the neck, before topping the ensemble with her woollen hat and scarf. The snow crunched under her feet as she set out for the Base, every step bringing with it a shiver of apprehension, as she tried to anticipate how her second meeting with Bo and Louie would go.

She could hear Carols being sung in the Canteen by some of

the duty personnel as she passed, before finally, reaching the Wing Commanders Quarters.

She was about to knock, when the door flew open and Louie ran out to greet her, followed by Bo.

"Lexie," he shouted, as he rushed into her arms, "You've come!"

Lexie couldn't help but grin at the boy's enthusiastic welcome and giggled as he took her hand and pulled her through the doorway.

"Come and see what Santa brought me," he rushed, "and Papa says we've got the biggest goose in Scotland to eat and this......." he turned breathlessly, "this is for you."

He handed Lexie a small parcel, his eyes gleaming with excitement.

Lexie felt a surge of panic.  She hadn't brought any gifts for the boy and here he was giving her a present.

She looked at Bo, her eyes asking for understanding.

"Santa left it under the tree," he said, shrugging his shoulders and grinning, "so you've got him to thank."

"Tell Santa thank you very much," Lexie whispered, her fingers holding the gift gently in her hands, "but I'll open it later, if that's alright" she added, dropping the parcel into her handbag, "once we've eaten that huge goose Louie talked about."

Bo nodded, she had come and, for now, that was enough.

"C'mon then you two," he said, brightening, "let's see what Uncle Martin's left for us in the dining room.  Louie needed no second telling and rushed through to the laden table.  "Thanks Lexie," Bo said, quietly, as he escorted her to her chair, "Louie would have been miserable if you hadn't come.......and.... so would I."

Lexie felt a rush of colour tinge her cheeks, as Bo pulled back the chair for her to sit but, again, couldn't find her voice to speak.

The lunch was superb.  How Martin Kettlewell had managed to arrange such a feast for them, Lexie couldn't imagine.  The goose was, indeed, enormous and succulent and the Christmas

Pudding that followed was spiced with cinnammon and rich with fruit.

A bottle of red wine was drank, with Louie having Raspberry Cordial to toast Christmas and a peace had settled over everyone before Lexie realised darkness had began to fall again.

She glanced at Louie, playing with his toy airplane and pretending he was a pilot like his dad. "I'd best be going," she said, visualising her lonely walk home, "it'll be dark soon."

"Stay a while longer," Bo said, quickly, moving to sit beside her, "please."

"I'd like to," Lexie said, "but I don't....."

"It's alright," Bo told her, "I know you weren't expecting to see me again, but now you have, I only ask one thing...."

Lexie's eyes met his, dark and compelling. "We fly back home tomorrow," he said, his voice breaking, "but me and Louie would like it very much if we could write to you and maybe you could write back?"

The question hung in the air between them, as memories of meeting Bo for the first time at Lossiemouth flashed into her mind.

"Am I asking too much?" Bo added, "I hope not."

Lexie finally found her voice, as time seemed to warp and only that moment seemed to count.

"I'd like that Bo," she said, shyly, "and I will write back, I promise."

Bo squeezed her hand. "And when Lexie Melville promises something, I know she keeps it."

Bo wanted to take her in his arms and carry her off to Canada with him, but he knew it was too soon but over time, somehow, he would convince Lexie to give him another chance to love her.

"Can I walk you home?" Bo asked, helping Lexie to her feet, "don't want you getting lost in the wilds of Montrose," he grinned, hoping for a little more time with her.

"I'll be fine," she said, "and say goodbye to Louie for me, he's a lovely boy," she added, "just like his Papa."

Bo nodded, accepting that this time together would have to be enough for now, but the future, well, that was still to be written, letter by letter.

Home in her room, Lexie opened her Christmas gift from Santa.

Inside the wrapping was a small box and inside the box was the little wooden ring that Bo had given her when they first realised they were in love. It had belonged to his mother and was carved with Red Indian symbols. Lexie felt a tear form in the corner of her eye as she slipped the ring back onto her finger.

"Write soon," she whispered aloud, "very soon." Maybe love had found Lexie again after all.

# Chapter 31

The horror of Billy's anger on Christmas Eve was still reverberating through Nancy's system as she awoke from a fitful night's sleep. The memory of his last words as he pushed past her and John Brannan filled her heart. 'SLUT' he'd called her, the venom in the word still making her recoil.

Shakily, she swapped the warmth of her bed for the coldness of the dark kitchen. Thankfully, Mary Anne, wee Billy and Kevin slept on as Nancy pulled a heavy cardigan around her shoulders and set about rekindling the fire. At least they had been unaware of Billy's visit and would be able to enjoy the Christmas dinner she had planned for them.

The fire began to catch and Nancy filled the kettle at the kitchen sink, squinting through the frosted window to see that more snow had fallen overnight. Shivering, she made herself some tea and took it to her chair by the struggling fire, her fingers wrapped around the hot cup.

Christmas morning, she thought to herself, her mind going back to Christmases past when life with Billy had been good. Mary Anne and wee Billy had been bairns then and were now grown and King Kevin hadn't even been born when it had all started to go wrong.

If only, Nancy pondered wearily, if only Gladys Kelly had never existed, they would still be a family and Billy would be here, sharing Christmas with them. She shook her head to disperse the notion, accepting that Billy had returned to the prostitute time and again, despite her father's warnings. "SLUT" she said aloud, gazing at the fire, "is that what I am?"

She poured herself more tea and returned to her chair. For

Nancy, Jim Murphy was to be a husband to her and father to her bairns, but all he really wanted was to bed her. She felt a tear begin to form and blinked it away.

"NO!" she told herself firmly, "no man would ever fool her again, not Jim Murphy nor Billy Donnelly nor anyone else."

This Christmas Day was the first day of her new life and she'd face it alone, resolving that living for her bairns and herself was all she wanted and needed.

As the light crept into the kitchen, a flash of white on the floor beside the door caught Nancy's eye. She picked up a folded piece of paper and opened it.

Forgive me Nancy, she read, I'll wait for you at the Wellgate Steps. Without you, I have nothing to live for.

It was signed by Billy and Nancy felt a wave of fear hit her as she reread the words. Without you, I have nothing to live for.

John Brannan opened the curtains of his home at the same time as Nancy read Billy's note and looked down on the snow-covered Cowgate. The blanket of white had covered the grime and slush of the day before but clearly marked in the snow were heavy-booted footprints leading to Nancy's close. Anxiously, he threw open the window for a closer look. He'd kept a vigil till gone midnight, but sometime after that, someone had made their way to Nancy's home and John was under no illusion as to who that someone might be.

With his heart thudding, he rushed out into the street, but just as he began running to Nancy's home he spotted a second set of identical footprints on the other side of the road, this time heading away from her door. John took a deep breath, Billy Donnelly had come back, but it also looked like he'd gone again.

His common sense began to kick in and his breathing steadied. If Nancy had been harmed, he would have heard a commotion and surely, one of her bairns would have come and got him.

He looked up at Nancy's window, there was a faint light shining out but there was no sound of distress. Relief washed over him as he went back inside, everything was alright, he assured himself and now, surely, even Billy Donnelly would realise that any thoughts of getting back to Nancy were doomed.

Billy stamped his frozen feet and wrapped his arms around his lanky frame.  The sky was leaden and it looked like even more snow would fall that day, but he knew his only chance of getting back with Nancy was if he had stirred enough fear and guilt in her with his words, that she came looking for him.

He'd just have to wait it out and hope.

Nancy read the words again and the fear that Billy would take his own life, indeed, filled her heart. And would she really be to blame, she asked herself, if he did?  If she hadn't gone to bed with Jim Murphy........?  But even as she thought it, she knew it was Billy's obsession with the prostitute that had wrecked their marriage, not Jim Murphy......but still?

She glanced at the ticking clock.  Almost nine!  If she left now, she could be back within the hour and Christmas could begin proper and her conscience would be clear.

Wrapping herself up against the cold and with a thick woollen shawl pulled around her head and neck, Nancy crept out of the house and into the street.  Billy's footprints could be clearly seen and she stepped into them to keep the worst of the snow off her boots, almost falling as she tried to match the length of his stride. It wasn't far to the Wellgate Steps but it took longer than Nancy had anticipated and by the time she was struggling up the steep cobbled road, she was hot and angry.

Tears had begun to course down her cheeks.  "How dare Billy do this to her," she muttered to herself, "she didn't want him DEAD, she only wanted him OUT OF HER LIFE!"

Billy watched as Nancy struggled through the snow, smiling to himself as her slithering steps brought her nearer to him.

She was his again and he knew it.

John Brannan watched from his window as Nancy made her way past. She could only be venturing out for one reason and that reason was Billy Donnelly.  He slumped into his chair, Nancy must still love the man, he decided, resignation sitting heavily on his shoulders, despite everything that had happened, he just had to snap his fingers and she went running. He poked the fire, sending a shower of sparks up the chimney. Billy Dawson would have to be told, that despite everything he'd tried to do to keep her safe, his daughter had returned to her husband and there was nothing either of them could do about it.

All around them the streets were deserted as Nancy faced Billy.

"Well, she said, anger rising at the sight of him, "still alive?"

She'd taken the bait and Billy reached out to bring her closer, but Nancy backed away, pulling the shawl tighter.

"Only if you tell me there's a chance for us to forget the past and begin a new life together," he whined, "you know, forgive and forget!"

Nancy gazed at Billy's dishevelled state and gaunt features. The man she'd fallen in love with all those years ago was gone and had been replaced by this stranger. Whether it had been down to the war or the past, Nancy no longer knew, but whatever it was, she felt herself recoil from the sight of him. She knew now for certain that she could no more love him again than she could accept his bedding of Gladys Kelly.

The tears had dried in the cold air of Christmas morning as Nancy took another step away from her husband. "Too much water has gone under the bridge," she said, stonily, "and there's no way back for us."

Billy flinched. What was she saying!

"You can't mean that," he said, desperation gripping him......
"I'll kill myself" he said, "you know I will..."

But Nancy's heart had hardened to Billy's pleading. "I hope not," she said and she meant it, but she no longer felt responsible for his future, she only knew it was never going to be with her and the bairns.

She could hear him calling her name again and again as she made her way back down the steps and into the Wellgate, but her determination never faltered as she walked away, nor did she turn around. All fear of Billy and what he might do had left her, from now on she would live her life alone.

Billy stood watching till Nancy disappeared. His last ruse had failed and there was only one option left to him. He walked down Meadowside and into Bell Street. "If she thought I'd kill myself because of her," he muttered to himself, anger now replacing any remorse he'd felt as he stood in the snow waiting for Nancy to come to his rescue, "then she was sadly mistaken."

His steps quickened as he neared Bell Street Jail, but the entrance to the Jail was shut and barred. Billy looked for another way in, but there was none. He stepped back from the door and began to laugh…. but the laughter was soon replaced by deep sobs, as he realised that he wasn't even welcome at a prison! The last of his energy suddenly ebbed and he dropped down into the snow, "tomorrow," he murmured to himself, warmth beginning to seep into his frozen body, "he'd see Sergeant Murchison tomorrow, join up again…….be a man….." he told himself, before sleep overcame him.

Billy would be found the next day by Sergeant Murchison, frozen to death in the snow.

Nancy turned into the Cowgate after her meeting with Billy, determined to make the most delicious Christmas Dinner for her family. Billy Donnelly wouldn't trouble her again, she told herself, firmly, and if he did, she'd soon sort him out! Her confidence was high and nothing or no one was going to ruin this Christmas Day.

"Are you alright Nancy," the anxious voice of John Brannan asked. He'd been watching out for her return and had hurried down the stairs to meet her.

Nancy stopped short. "Mr Brannan," she said tightly, remembering their last encounter, when he'd let slip that her father had asked him to look after her in his absence. "You can report to my father that all is well," she said, briskly, "my husband won't be back to bother me again, so you don't have to watch over me anymore."

John flinched. She wasn't meant to know about the arrangement, but now she did, it looked like he'd deceived her, just like Billy Donnelly had done.

"I'm sorry, Nancy," he said, quietly, "I would have protected you even if your father hadn't asked me to."

Nancy's eyes narrowed. She didn't know that to make of this man and memories of Jim Murphy and his sweet words, that meant nothing at all, filled her mind.  Was she misjudging John Brannan because of the past?

"Apology accepted," she said, "now if you don't mind, I have a chicken to cook."

With that, Nancy turned away, leaving John in the cold.

"Maybe I could be your first foot at New Years?" he called after her, unable to think of anything else to say to keep her attention a little longer.

"Maybe," Nancy called over her shoulder before disappearing into the close.

John Brannan felt his heart rise in his chest.  "Maybe," he repeated, softly, turning to climb the stairs to home, "maybe is enough."

# Chapter 32

The boat trip to Belfast was going smoothly, despite the December weather and Annie and Billy couldn't wait to be reunited with their son, Dr John Adams.

"Are you happy, Annie?" Billy asked, as they sat in the tiny cabin, a tray of tea and sandwiches between them, supplied by the ship's Steward.

Annie's eyes glistened. "Lexie's settled in Montrose," she said "and, thanks to you, Nancy's in her new home and safe from another visit from Billy Donnelly."

Her husband nodded, "I know that, Annie," he said, "but are you happy with me and with our son?" Annie reached out for Billy's hand. "I've never been happier than I was on the day we met and I fell in love with this handsome stranger."

Billy relaxed, "nor I, Annie," he said, lovingly, "nor I."

It was Annie who saw him first, as they embarked from the Steamer at Belfast. He was the image Billy had been at that age and Annie felt a surge of pride.

"MUM," John Adams waved furiously from behind the dock barrier, "OVER HERE."

With her hand firmly clutched in Billy's they hurried towards John.

The barrier was pushed aside by a dock worker to let them through and with much smiling and hugging, the trio were re-united.

John had been taken away from Annie at his birth, by the nuns in the poorhouse in Belfast and sent to be adopted by a Doctor and his wife.

Annie thought she'd never see her son again, but Bella, her

only friend at that time, had managed to find out where John had gone and even managed to get work as a Scullery Maid in the house, keeping an eye on Annie's son as he grew up and writing to her about him.

But one day, Annie had received a letter from her son, wanting to come to Dundee to meet her. The pair met and John not only met his mother for the first time, but later discovered his real father was Billy Dawson. And now, all three were together for the first time.

"The motor's just outside the dock gates," John said "and there's a hot meal.....and a dram or two," he winked at Billy, "waiting at home." But that wasn't the only thing waiting at John's house. The door was opened by a lovely young woman, a cascade of dark curls framing her face and two startlingly blue eyes that shone a welcome.

Annie and Billy were ushered into the warm hallway where they removed their coats, while John went back to the car to retrieve their suitcases.

"Something smells good, Mary," he said, sniffing the air, as he deposited the bags in the hall. Mary grinned, "Irish Stew," she said, "to welcome your Mammy and Daddy."

Annie had to smile at the words, it was what she herself used to call her own mother and father, all those years ago on the farm outside Belfast.

"How lovely of you," Annie beamed, hugging the girl warmly, "I had a sister called Mary, you know, so it's great to hear the name again and, from one so beautiful."

Mary blushed sweetly as John slipped his arm around her shoulder.

His mother had taken to Mary almost instantly and he could see that his father, too, had been smitten by her.

The stew was delicious, with a bottle of red wine to wash it down and a dram for Billy later, as they sat in the Parlour before a blazing fire. Annie and Billy were regaled with John's stories of hospital life and how he'd met Mary as she nursed his patients back to health and Billy, in turn, updated their son on 'the goings on' in Dundee and Baxters and the lives of Lexie and

Nancy in particular.

And it was late into the evening when John cleared his throat and called for silence as he had an announcement to make.  His eyes glistened as he looked at his mother and father, marvelling at how fate had brought them all together.

He took Mary's hand and helped her to her feet. "Mum, Dad," he said, nodding to each in turn, "two days from now, on the 23rd of December," me and Mary are to be married….." Annie gasped into the sudden hush, before bursting into tears of joy. "MARRIED!" she echoed, grasping Billy's hand for support, "and to the beautiful Mary."

The four of them collapsed in laughter and happiness. "And," John added "as Mary has no daddy of her own," he turned to Billy, a seriousness creeping into his voice, "will you walk with her down the aisle?"

Billy glowed.  "Nothing would give me more pleasure," he said, "if Mary will allow me?" he added, already knowing by her smile that she would.

"And mum," John continued, will you be our Maid of Honour?"

Annie was lost for words and could only nod vigorously.

"Then it's agreed," John said, "This is going to be the most wonderful wedding day ever.

The following two days were a hive of industry, as everyone lent a hand making the final arrangements for the couple to be married in their local church.  Despite rationing and shortages, the wedding cake was miraculously produced by the nurses at the hospital and Mary's dress was fashioned by her mum, a skilled seamstress.

The sun shone brightly against a deep blue winter sky as Billy escorted Mary down the aisle, before Annie took her place alongside the bride.

To tears all round, the Minister pronounced the couple, husband and wife before John kissed his new bride to the delight of their families and friends.   The Church Hall had been decked out for the Reception and the merriment went on till the hour was late, but eventually, everyone waved off the happy pair to a 'secret location' outside Belfast for their two day honeymoon.

"See you both on Christmas Day" John called out to his parents, as he guided Mary into his motorcar. "Christmas Day it is," answered Billy, his arm around Annie's shoulder keeping her warm in the night air.

"Will they be happy?" Annie asked, tears misting her eyes, as the car disappeared around a corner.

"They will," Billy told her, pulling her closer to him, "I've never been so sure of anything in all my life," he added, "except my love for you darling girl."

The two days rushed by and before Annie knew it John and Mary were hurrying up to the front door, their arms linked together.

"Merry Christmas," John grinned, brushing snow from his coat, "and that goes for Mrs Adams too." Mary nudged her husband and blushed, not yet used to being called Mrs Adams.

Almost instantly, the aromas of baking and a roasting chicken swirled around them. Annie had been busy, as usual, preparing their Christmas Dinner and welcome home feast at the same time, while Billy had secured a Christmas tree and had draped it with tinsel and glittering fairy lights, which he'd been assured by the shopkeeper 'won't burst into flames.'

"It's beautiful," Mary whispered in awe of the tree and the table set for four, the cutlery gleaming in the glow of three candles, sitting on a bed of holly berries and ivy leaves, that Annie had woven around them.

Annie's cooking skills had excelled and it was amidst murmurs of delight and nods of thanks in her direction, that the soup was supped and the platefuls of roast fowl and potatoes and wonderful gravy were eaten.

"A toast," Billy said, raising his glass and standing and everyone followed suit. "To the happy couple," he said, clinking glasses all round "and to the merriest Christmas in all the land."

Then it was John's turn. "To the most wonderful 'mammy' and 'daddy' in the world," he said, "and to absent friends past and present."

Memories of Annie's late sister, Mary, Euan's son, Ian, in Carlisle with his new wife, Joe Cassiday, now also long gone and Lexie and Nancy, filled Annie's mind.  "To absent friends," she whispered, "past and present."

Billy knew what she was thinking.  He too remembered his ex- wife, Josie McIntyre and his daughters, still living in Dundee and the time and place his love for Annie  had all begun, The year was 1900 in that little farm outside Belfast, when he and Annie had first met.  It was now 1946 and two world wars had happened in that time, along with all the changes to both of their lives and those of their children.

"And to the future," Mary added her toast quietly, "may it be all we wish for."

"I think we all second that," John said, kissing her gently on the forehead "and before we clear the table and get some sleep, let's take some time to just sit by the fire and thank God for the Lord's  birthday that has brought us all together again."

"That was lovely," Annie said, nestling into Billy's arms as they lay in bed together, "Will the future be alright," she asked, her voice a little sleepy and soft.

"It will, Annie," Billy replied, "it will."

And for Billy Dawson and Annie Pepper, the future was alright for the rest of their days on earth.

www.ingramcontent.com/pod-product-compliance
Lightning Source LLC
Chambersburg PA
CBHW070951120726
47910CB00004B/1191